Here's what some Sarasota
booksellers have to say after
previewing "Sarasota Bay"

"A true page-turner, nice mix of
suspense and humor."

(Deborah Logan)

"Quirky and believable characters
and a new view of Sarasota."

(Nancy Foust)

"... an enjoyable romp ..."

(Michele Waldock)

"Rushton finally found his niche!"

(Micki Slattery)

This book is dedicated to the Sarasota Police Department, who are neither buffoons, nor in the least bit 'Keystone' (as imaginary officers may be portrayed herein). They are instead a serious and tightly knit force that provides a safe & marvelous place to live and be creative.

Both author and publisher will donate a portion of all proceeds from all printings of this book to: Safe Place and Rape Crisis Center, Sarasota, FL.

My sincerest gratitude to LIDO Press, Inc. and the guidance of their wonderful editorial staff: Susana Falcon & Mary Lee Slettehaugh.

Also, I wish to thank those first few readers who saw the beauty within the mess, continued to read about Tyler, and asked for more, even if it meant more typewriter noise in the next room!

Sarasota Bay

BY

Rushton Woodside

Published by: LIDO press, Inc.

Copyright © 2004 Rushton Woodside
Cover photo, design, and setup © 2004 Rushton Woodside

Published by LIDO Press, Inc., Sarasota, Florida.

Library of Congress Cataloging-In-Publication data pending.

Manufactured in the United States of America.

ISBN 0-9762936-09

FIRST EDITION – November 2004

10 9 8 7 6 5 4 3 2 1

Chapter 01

Four gunshots echoed through the large room amplified by the terrazzo floors, the sliding glass doors, and the high ceiling. Acrid smells of gunpowder mixed with the coppery scent of fresh blood nearly overwhelmed the shooter.

Running to the door, the man stuffed the hot gun into the right pocket of his sports coat. Outside, he ran left onto the sidewalk, thinking that was the way out of the subdivision. He had no time to search the house for keys and take a car. The taxi that dropped him off at the house had left almost an hour ago.

His docksiders were not designed for running, made especially difficult in the dark by the sidewalk's twists and turns. He heard only the sound of his shoes slapping loudly against the concrete along the luxuriously landscaped right of way.

He was almost sick with regret from actually shooting someone. Gunshots weighed heavily on his conscience and their echoes pounded through his brain.

As his blazer flopped around, the gun slapped him in the back, and he tried not to cry out each time. He passed over a little wooden oriental bridge, and the hollow boom of each step reminded him again of the sounds lingering in his memory. He stopped, froze, held onto the handrail in a panic ... listened. The quiet drove him on again.

When he came to a darkened intersection, he was winded and disoriented. He faltered, then chose to go left, towards the beach, not into the city - not into civilization. Another intersection: lights to the right and a bridge to the left. Again he went left, onto the bridge, tripped on the dip of a driveway entrance, and fell to his hands and knees. But the man jumped immediately back onto his feet and limped up to the apex of the bridge, where he stopped and leaned against the metal railing, gasping for breath.

He watched his hat fall to the water as he drooped his head to stare mindlessly down, the yacht club insignia a sudden reminder of the reality of the situation he'd just left: the hot gun, the blood, the other man collapsing to the floor before he'd completed his second move, which would have been a flat handed chop to the neck. The shooter barely had time to pull the thirty-eight from the waistband of his pants and fire after receiving the first blow, to his solar plexus. At such a close range, the first shot did the trick. The other bullets were panic driven, causing most of the mess.

His eyes were closed tightly during the reflex shots that followed the kill shot. After owning the gun for thirty years, finally using it that way was a shock. It had only served as a threat in the past and, at worst, had been fired into the air.

No sirens yet... He caught his breath enough to run again and limped awkwardly down the slope of the bridge, onto yet another winding sidewalk. He passed between the rows of darkened mansions. The sound of his flopping shoe leather echoed all around him.

With no idea where he was, the short blocks went by rapidly. None of the houses seemed to offer any hiding places. They were all fenced, walled, gated, foreboding. He noticed a variety of security service signs. A large dog appeared behind one fence. Running hard to stay abreast, it barked furiously at him. This pushed the man to run harder and faster, his pains temporarily forgotten.

A few blocks later, the street changed from a divided boulevard to a simple two lane and ended at a cross street. To the right stood several high-rise condominiums and lots of bright streetlights and signs. On his left, a darkened park entrance beckoned: sanctuary and safety beyond. Again, he turned left, tripped, and limped down the dark lane.

With all the left turns, he knew it would be easy to work his way back to town when he was ready to do so. Better than a trail of bread crumbs, he thought, always turn to the right.

The park would serve as his hideout until daylight, when he'd call his partner to come and pick him up. All would end well, even without the ten thousand dollars he never took from the wall safe.

Chapter 02

Over Sarasota Bay, a pre-dawn glow was beginning to appear and the air was cooling, due to the heat of the Atlantic Ocean pushing the moist swamp air across the state to the gulf coast, typical for the middle of May.

Flowers were opening for business, wafting heavy sweet smells into the damp morning.

A pair of mourning doves awoke, adding sound to sight and smell. A well-versed mockingbird was beginning its litany, foretelling the imminent sunrise. A random splash and rustling noises in the mangroves lining the shore indicated that another night in paradise was coming to an end in the usual graceful manner.

Tyler Polk silently trolled past Otter Key while he fished for snook as the beauty played on. But the morning symphony was suddenly marred by something off-key.

An echoing sound tattooed its way into his mind. Softly at first, but then quickly louder, he heard what seemed to be the sound of a tennis match played way too fast. The beats were not consistent though. One beat missed here, two there, a sudden staccato, silence, and then a sound as if someone were hitting the hull of a dry-docked wooden boat with a rubber mallet. Baffled, Tyler killed the trolling motor to eliminate the sound of the water that gurgled past the bow, and listened intently. Years of boredom living a stable life on a resort island had his curiosity piqued.

Realization finally came to him. Someone was running very fast in shoes not designed for running, and had just crossed the wooden bridge that led off of Otter Key towards St. Armand's Circle. Many of the locals were joggers, but rarely at four a.m., and always in proper footwear.

An accomplished woodsman from an early age, Tyler was able to pinpoint the location of the runner, gauge the speed, and even deduce that it was a tall person running to the max. The person slowed where Mangrove Lane intersected with South Washington Boulevard and then took off again at full speed, headed towards the beaches.

Tyler kicked the foot control of the trolling motor onto full and followed at a speed that he felt would quickly catch him up to any runner. He reeled in his fishing line, carefully stowed the rod, and then retrieved his night vision binoculars from their case.

The sound grew suddenly louder as he neared the bridge that crossed to South Lido Key, so he again shut the motor down. While coasting to a stop he focused on the bridge and was immediately rewarded with the sight of a man who stumbled up the bridge, then stopped to lean over the railing while gasping for breath. The man's hat fell to the water below, and he slumped on the metal rail for support.

The runner coughed and spat into the water, cussed loudly, then took off on a run again with his jacket flapping in his wake. Tyler now felt certain that nothing was right about this whole situation, that the man had not been jogging off to a neighbor's house for breakfast.

Tyler cranked up his outboard motor this time, surged toward the floating hat and expertly swooped it into the boat with his hand net before the water was disturbed by his wake.

After a quick turn, the boat was on a plane and headed south. He was suddenly in pursuit of this random runner, if only to return the lost hat to its rightful owner. Lido was so heavily policed on a year round basis that danger never entered his mind.

Assuming that the man was headed towards the park at the south end of the key, Tyler went straight there and beached the boat between two clumps of mangrove roots, tied off hurriedly, and crept into the woods at the edge of the parking lot, in case that was the destination. Just as he was settled in, he heard the man come towards him.

In the glow of the streetlights he saw the man pause at the park entrance, trip over the chain the rangers put up at night, and then limp awkwardly down the main drive. He slowed, grunting with each step, came to the turn-around, collapsed onto a bench no more than ten feet away from Tyler, doubled over, clutched his knees in both hands, and rocked slowly.

This allowed Tyler the chance to creep a little further back into the underbrush. The proximity of the man and the heavy breathing had gotten Tyler's adrenaline pumping at a critical level. He was now more scared than curious, and was beginning to doubt the sanity of staying so close.

What he saw was a paunchy middle-aged man, with gray hair at the temples, who wore a messy and torn white linen suit and boating shoes, which accounted for the clumsy and noisy running.

As Tyler stared, he saw that there were splatters of dark red on the man's coat and trousers. Tyler figured the spots were not from a skinned knee, but there was no indication as to whether they were the man's own or someone else's. A serious injury had obviously taken place.

The man suddenly jumped up and limped off into the woods, while cussing under his breath with each step. Concern over the possibility that the man was the victim of something terrible over-ruled fear that he was some sort of criminal, so Tyler resisted the urge to get the hell out of there, and decided to follow him deeper into the park instead, spot his hiding place, and then call the police.

It was easy to tail the man as he splashed his way through a little canal that wound through the swamp. Tyler stayed far behind and just followed the noise deep into the preserve, the territory of mangrove snakes, rabid raccoons, feral possums, and filthy fruit rats. Though the park encompassed almost a hundred acres, there was no concern over getting lost, as he had traveled through all of it on foot, bike, or canoe at one time or another over the years.

It was easy to take the time to walk carefully along the edge of the mangrove forest while stepping from root to root, because he knew their destination. There was a small tidal lake sequestered in the center of the park where all of the various canoe trails converged, and it was the only place for the man to go and find some semblance of ground.

Within a few minutes Tyler found himself crouched behind a palmetto palm at the edge of the lake, watching the man struggle across the water, half swimming and half walking, then clambering up the opposite bank to collapse into a large thicket of yellow Thumbergia.

Tyler waited for his pulse and breathing to slow, and for his scrambled mind to reassemble itself into a flow of reasonable thinking. Things stayed quiet long enough for an osprey to start hunting for breakfast, swoop down into the lake, splash loudly on impact, then squawk furiously as it flew back into the adjacent forest with a struggling fish in its claws.

No human movement or sound was evident from the thicket for a good while, so he eventually headed back the way he had come, this time making enough noise of his own to keep the local critters at bay.

Once in the boat, still shaking, he fumbled with the key in the ignition and startled a family of wild green parrots into beginning the usual morning bitching session early. The continual loud screams of the birds wore on his nerves as he backed out of the shelter of the trees and hurried home, back to the sanity of his dockhouse on the key, wondering all the way what he would say to the police when he called. A slight bit of paranoia hit him when he thought about the fact that he might be questioned as a possible suspect, or as an accomplice to a crime.

Chapter 03

The first rays of sunrise lit up some low clouds as Tyler backed the bass boat into the dockhouse at five am, an early return for him on a Sunday. As usual, he stopped at the mirror, saw the standard wind swept imitation of Bill Gates, and spent a few minutes to get his thick, curly, sandy brown hair back into some semblance of order.

He unlocked a padlock and opened the hasp to let himself into the large storage room that served as home on those rare occasions when he wasn't outside. After he swung out the two screen-less windows and propped them open with some boards against the sea breeze that would soon begin, Tyler collapsed into his one chair, an expensive leather Barca-Lounger that looked decidedly out of place against the cypress planked floor.

After he calmed down a bit, Tyler decided that it seemed ludicrous to call the police with no real information to report. So he switched on his rarely used television and changed from the Weather Channel to ABC-7 to see if there was any breaking local news which might correspond to what he had seen. There was nothing but the usual droll Sarasota news: one auto accident, another day in paradise weather wise, yet another recipe-of-the-day being prepared by a local chef, and all of the newscasters yumming over another free breakfast.

Unable to shake his curiosity, he decided that if he were to find out anything more, it would have to be from the only source: the possible fugitive in the woods.

Tyler eyed his collection of spy-ware from the Sharper Image catalog (most of which had only been used previously for attracting dust), grabbed a few select items and added them to the cycling pack which was always by the door to the landside of the dockhouse. It was time to do some 'double-ought' spying, he thought, and smiled for the first time that day. A little distance between him and the man would certainly make things safer.

He removed a different padlock from the front door to let himself out, used that lock to secure the door to the boat area from the inside, and went onto the main dock where a third padlock hung on a nail waiting to be used to secure things from the outside.

Everyone that he had met since moving to Lido made fun of that arrangement, but he always explained that it came that way when he bought the place, suited him fine, and even reminded him of the barns back home.

A brief bike ride down Ben Franklin Drive ended at one of the park's side trails, one that skirted the western edge of the lake where his 'John Doe' would hopefully still be hiding. After stopping at what seemed about the right spot, Tyler locked up the bicycle, slipped into the edge of the woods, and scanned the embankment that led down to the edge of the lake. The quickly rising sun made it difficult to see to the east, but he finally spotted a conspicuous flash of white through the scraggly Australian pines clustered at the edge of the water.

From the pack he produced the small pocket fishing rig that he always kept in a side pocket, and his miniature wireless microphone that would transmit to any FM radio. Fumbling hands tied the mic to the fishing line, but a practiced cast sent it between the trees where it landed fairly close to the man's inert form.

Tyler laid the rod down, quietly covered it with some loose leaves, and dug out his armband radio. He used this combination frequently to amplify birdcalls, so the radio was already set to the correct frequency required to receive signals from the little transmitter. He heard nothing but light static, so as a test, he threw a small stick down the hill and heard it land in the underbrush. The man also heard the stick, and groaned, causing Tyler's already strained breathing to catch and his heart to jump. He backed down the path, but after a few steps noticed that he had forgotten the backpack. He quickly decided to leave it, and nearly ran on tiptoe back to the sidewalk where the bike was chained to a street sign. As he mounted up, he remembered that he'd have to stay within about fifty yards to maintain reception, and nearly decided to ditch the whole plan. But again, an early retiree's boredom spurred him on.

After riding to the head of the next trail, he pulled in and waited, shook slightly as he sat on the bike seat, ready to take off if need be.

He heard another groan in his ears, a cough, rustling noises, and then the loudest profanity he had ever heard: "DAMNIT, I can't believe dat went so wrong!"

There was a long stream of coughs, and then: "What now!" - more of a moan than a question.

Tyler finally realized he had not really thought everything through properly. He was eavesdropping on a bloody man who was only one wind sprint away, and was apparently pretty agitated.

Suddenly the voice came through again: "Sue, thank God you woke up an' answered. Lissen: not only didn't it work, it's worse than I woulda guessed it would evah get. I got him to agree to pay, an' he was openin' a wall safe, an' whattaya think, he frigging turned on me wit some kinda fancy karate shit. Now I'm lost in da woods somewheres an' soaking wet an' I hurt my leg. But he didn't get me an' he's dead now an' I ain't got da money. I showed him da pictures an' he really bugged out his eyes, bitchin' an' moanin' about don't tell his wife, an' was gonna pay but I hadda shoot him an' he's dead."

Tyler massaged the temples of his lowered head during the pause, and was back to shaking all over again when he heard the man continuing.

"Shaddup ya bitch. Doncha go freakin' on me. Lissen, I'm here on one a dese islands, dressed in dis gooney suit an' yer all high and dry."

Another pause. "You gotta come get me but I dunno exactly where I am an' dese clothes are a mess. Lotsa blood. He's friggin' dead an' ya gotta wait until dark but ya gotta come get me den."

Tyler knew that he would be calling the police soon and handing this over to them. The wave of calmness that passed over him felt incredible.

The man spoke again, starting to yell: "Whattaya mean, no? Yer in dis as deep as me. Deeper even, ya know, cause I got da pictures wit YOU an' HIM together, and dey show YOUR innit all da way cause he's married an' YOU ain't his wife. I could just mailem to da cops an' YOU'D be screwed big time. Dey'd think YOU offed him, but dey don't know WHO I AM! Dey don't know WHERE I AM AT!"

The man's anger was more than Tyler had ever witnessed. He knew that there was a whole world 'out there' that he would just as soon stop experiencing. The voice came back once more.

"Lissen. SHADDUP! HEY LISSEN! Hey woman, ya still dere? HEY! ... SHIT!"

There was a lot of underbrush noise next, but Tyler was frozen in place, eyes clamped shut, still holding his head. Then a voice right beside him: "Hey Mister. Are you okay?"

Tyler jerked into an upright position and lost his hold on the bike. It fell to an angle between his legs and the teeth of the crank scraped his right calf. His hands shot straight up into the air and he cried out tentatively. Then he slowly opened his eyes to see a family who had been walking down the trail.

"Mister, do you need me to call 911?" asked the father. "You look like you're having a heart attack or something."

After Tyler somehow managed a reply about a song on the radio reminding him of an old girlfriend, he picked up the bike and explained that they ought to go back the way they had just come from, since there was a downed tree blocking the trail ahead. The last thing he wanted was for an innocent family to get hurt by being in the mystery man's way.

They all looked at the obviously clear path then back at Tyler. The man touched his wife's elbow and led them back along the trail, casting one last concerned glance back over his shoulder.

The rustling noises continued, but not the sound of brush being trampled upon ... yet. What to do? Call the police now? The man might be moving soon. Better for Tyler to wait another couple of minutes to be sure he could tell them exactly where the man was, and even who had been killed and where. Tyler had witnessed nothing illegal and had no proof of a crime having been committed. Maybe the man would make another phone call so that Tyler could get the information he wanted.

The immediate answer seemed to be not to appear so conspicuous. He went back to the road, where he biked south about a hundred yards, stopped to waste time with some unnecessary stretching, and then headed slowly north to do the same again. On his second such round, the voice came back.

"Lissen Sue. It's Tony again. I'm leavin' ya dis one message, an' it's come over dis way out to da islands. Call me when ya get here an' we'll figger out where to meet. Come on NOW, we don't havta wait until dark 'cause I've got da blood kinda covered up. I need ya baby. Call me right back."

This was followed by the noise of the man scrambling up the slope of the lake bank. Obviously, he was on the move again. As Tyler rode, he spotted a newspaper box in front of a hotel and went to peer into it as if reading the headlines through the little window. The noises in his ear got fainter, became the crunching of shoes on the path, so he knew that 'Tony' had made it to the actual trail, and was skulking around in the park.

Sure enough, he emerged from the woods with his jacket casually draped over the right leg of his trousers to cover the blood, wearing just his undershirt. He glanced both ways, shrugged, and started walking south, away from Tyler.

The sun was fully up and the sidewalk had started to fill with real joggers, bikers, and dog walkers. The six am shift. Barring close inspection, Tony blended right in with the crowd.

Tyler hung back, knowing the road ended at the main portion of South Lido Park, less than a mile ahead. As the man walked, Tyler would sporadically ride a short way, then stop and pretend to inspect the front tire of the bike. He felt almost safe by following in this manner.

Towards the end of the road, he allowed himself time to catch up just at the entrance and bravely ride past the man into the park, heading into one of the more populated areas of the picnic grounds. Another tire inspection allowed him to see Tony heading towards a bench that was off by itself and empty - where he sat and crossed his arms over his chest and his legs at the ankles, looking for all the world like a local at the beach passing a casual morning watching the gulls harass the early picnickers.

Tyler took a similar pose nearby and waited, confident that he could get more information to pass on when he made his call.

Rushton Woodside

Chapter 04

Born Antonio Guissepe DeCastro Jr. in South Boston in 1944, Tony had it rough from the very beginning. His father was an itinerant laborer and his mother the daughter of the minister of the one Presbyterian Church in Southie. She had been taken by surprise with the way that Antonio Sr. had swept her off her feet at the North Shore one summer. Passing himself off as the owner of a fleet of lobster boats and as being descendant from Sicilian royalty, he seemed an unlikely match for her white-bread Protestant upbringing, but his mystique had been impossible for her to resist.

Him being so suave and soft-spoken, though, she felt she could trust his immediate and adamant claim of love at first sight. She did not know that

Antonio had no idea exactly who his ancestors might be - including his father - and that he had never been onboard a boat, much less learned to swim.

What Antonio knew at first sight was that Sarah Fifield came from money, and he always loved money at any sight, so his claim was sincere in its own right.

After a whirlwind courtship, they were married in the fall and he impregnated her with Junior. The new father-in-law provided money for an addition to the fleet as a wedding present and Antonio ran with the money, and is presumably still running.

She started calling Junior Tony to avoid any mental comparisons to his father. Though a troublesome child, he had enough conman in his blood to get his grandfather to lend him money to start a lobster boat painting business when he turned eighteen. He ran with it - and is obviously still running.

Tyler, born Tyler Harrison Polk on a farm near Flowery Branch, Georgia in 1952, conversely had it easy from the very beginning. He was born with a silver shovel in his mouth, one spoon in each hand, and a thick vein of silver running through the family property, directly above the bedrock.

His father had been a successful fourth generation cattle rancher and his mother was the only child of the preacher at the Praise Hallelujah

Congregational Church in nearby Acworth. They had courted for three years, and were engaged for another full year before their wedding.

Tyler came into the world a respectable fourteen months after the ceremony, and at eighteen years of age, was given the deed to a cattle ranch of his own in Sarasota, Florida. He eventually parlayed that land into over three hundred luxury home sites, set amidst slightly rolling terrain a few miles inland from the gulf beaches.

He respects money, but does not love it, or the spending thereof. He now owns three busy restaurants, a small chain of convenience stores, a car dealership, his beloved dockhouse, and another cattle ranch farther inland. Though he runs twice daily, it is always for his health, and never from anyone or anything.

These two disparate characters were sitting within fifty yards of each other with two opposing missions, and their thoughts were running intently in drastically different directions.

Rushton Woodside

Chapter 05

Tony's thoughts ran towards Susan - to how they had pulled this same scam two to three times a year since they met in Los Angeles a few years before. The main ingredient of the con was the costumes that they had perfected over the years. For him, it was a generic white linen suit with a similarly generic yacht club insignia on the breast pocket, and a scrambled-eggs type yachtsman's cap always worn at an absurd, jaunty angle. Susan wore a bikini, a handkerchief-sized tropical wraparound skirt with accompanying high-heeled sandals, and a killer tan. The couple bore a striking resemblance to Mr. Howell and Ginger Grant from Gilligan's Island.

Whenever cash ran out, the scam began with a trip to any gulf-coast city large enough to boast a yacht club. One or both of them would then get a job, any job, at the club and then scout out a suitable client. The right prospect would be married, of course, and would ignore his wife while flirting with any female within striking distance. This type of man would invariably spend time 'alone' on his boat with some frequency.

Timing was everything. Tony and Susan would stroll the docks at night as often as they could, looking just like they belonged, and were never suspected by virtue of being so out of context. Once the right situation was encountered, they would approach the client's boat and feign "Looking for Eugene" (or Larrimore, or whoever came to mind.)

After some confusion the usual drink offer would follow. Next Susan would complain of being tired of looking, and would wrangle an invitation to stay aboard, while Tony would leave to seek out the correct boat.

Susan never had a problem taking things from there. Proper placement of some Sharper Image gear of their own in her purse would invariably produce photos of her with the mark - and also the occasional visiting 'masseuse' as well - in some illicit and often multiple compromising positions.

The team thought of it as an eye for an eye, not as blackmail. If the man was willing to drift from his wife, he should have to pay for it at least twice. They were not stealing and not embezzling, just extracting a karmic payment from someone who could well afford it.

This was essentially how they had met in California. What Susan had not known was that Tony was not on his boat, not at his club, and not in possession of any money for the karmic gristmill.

He just had knowledge of who came and went at the Venice Beach Yacht Club, and was enjoying an extended stay on a well-stocked boat while the owner was in Jamaica. Susan had tried her stunt on Tony, and really didn't believe him at first when he confessed. After a week spent emptying the galley and the very well stocked medicine cabinet of all consumable products, they decided to partner up.

Now it was far easier for her to get in, and Tony provided a little strong-arm force if a client became obstinate when payoff time came along. They had yet to fail - that is, until the night before.

Trying again to call her, Tony got her voice mail once more. This time he left a simple and terse message for her to call him back. He knew she would. He knew that their team was the best there ever was; better than Bonnie & Clyde, since they never got chased, and - unlike Clyde - Tony could get it up and keep it going. Susan certainly wouldn't want to break up such a divine partnership over one little lost sale.

After making the call, he laid his cigarette lighter and last few cigarettes out on the bench beside him to dry in the sun. He sure needed a smoke. He sure needed her to show up and get him out of there before somebody found the mess he left behind. He had, as usual, taken a taxi in the middle of the night to collect, but hadn't left in a borrowed car, as he always did (most clients were so pleased to see him go they were happy to lend him transportation). He never kept the cars he borrowed - after all, that would be stealing. (This last client would never be pleased about anything again).

Tony hoped that the twenty he had given the cab driver was enough to keep him happy and quiet, and casually turned the cigarettes over, re-crossed his arms, waited.

Tyler, having forgotten in his excitement that he was no longer monitoring Tony's actions through the transmitter, mindlessly listened to the static on the radio, and also waited while watching the only family in the picnic area. They were local Mennonites, with the women wearing their little white caps and heavy dresses, the men in their home-made denim coveralls and straw hats. They had seemingly only forgotten the kitchen sink.

The raccoons did a double check of the garbage cans, and the seagulls stood on the beach while waiting patiently for the raccoons to go away.

A scattering of tourists slowly walked past and stopped here and there, picking at shells on the shoreline. The scene was so typical for an off-season morning that Tyler almost could have forgotten why he was there.

Time passed. He finally checked his watch and found that it was nearly seven thirty already, so he decided to call his nearly girlfriend, and certainly best friend, Kendra, to enlist some help in his aimless mission.

He received an out of breath answer: "Kendra!"

"Hey, it's me. Sounds like you're out blading."

"Yepper. Out cruising for the love of my life. Is that you yet, old man? I'm still waiting."

"Almost, as always. Hey, I'm at South Lido Park, in the middle of an interesting situation. Are you nearby, darling?"

"I could be soon," she purred. "What is an 'interesting situation'?"

"Hard to explain, since I'm not sure myself. Come on down, head left as you enter the park, and look for me on a bench. My yellow bike is leaning against the armrest."

"Sounds like a drug deal... or a password... I'm on my way. Give me about ten minutes, I'm just rounding the circle now, blue eyes."

"Okay, I'll explain when you get here. Bye."

"Bye bye, almost lover."

When Kendra arrived with her delicious smell of coconut oil and sweat, he told her what he knew. She listened very quietly throughout the whole explanation; then stood up, pulled him with her, grabbed him, and gave him a long kiss on the lips - with a full contact hug attached. As they broke away, her gold-flaked brown eyes bore holes into him as always.

"That's to help protect your cover," she explained.

He blushed and adjusted his shorts, but gave a straight reply: "I want you to wait here while I go get my car, and call me if he makes a move. Don't follow - just call."

"Sure, darling, but hurry, okay? This is just a little bit weird. I don't like the looks of your buddy over there."

"I'll be back soon. Don't follow - just call."

Within a few minutes, Tyler had thrown his ratty, yellow beach bike - and his guest bike - into the back of his old Toyota wagon and was headed back to the park when his cellphone rang.

He glanced at the caller ID and answered with: "Are you Okay?"

"Your guy just bartered a couple of cigarettes for a can of beer and is now strolling off down the beach towards the nature trails. What should I do?"

"Sit tight and take off your roller blades. I've put both bikes in the wagon and I'm almost there."

Kendra met him as he parked and pointed in the direction where Tony had gone. They hurriedly unloaded the bicycles and Tyler led the way down the trail that ran parallel to the beach. As they rode, she explained to him how a couple of homeless people had prompted the barter.

They rode until they could see Tony through the trees and then stopped. They leapfrogged along for a while like that, always staying behind him. He went all the way to the end of the beach where the mangroves choked off further access to the shoreline, and sat on the bench that was there.

Tyler picked out a safe spot for them to wait in the cover of an old live oak. They watched Tony chug the last of the beer, light a smoke, and make another call. Apparently, he got a live answer this time, as they could hear him yell into the phone, though could not quite make out what was being said. He made a lot of animated gestures with his free hand, and eventually stood up to assert himself.

It seemed that the conversation was not going to his liking. He finally held the phone at arm's length and screamed at it, as opposed to into it. They could clearly hear him now, cussing up a storm, as he made to throw the phone into the bay, but then checked himself at the last second.

"Looks like his partner has abandoned him," whispered Tyler.

"Good! Can we call the police now and go to the dockhouse to make some lovey dovey?"

"And tell them what? That I think somebody named Tony murdered somebody else over some money and pictures and that I don't know where or when or who?"

"That would work. Then the lovey dovey!"

"Ken, you know I'm against pre-marital lovey stuff and equally against marriage stuff. I need to find out more, somehow, before I make that call. It looks to me like Tony is stuck on the key, and I intend to keep an eye on him until I can find out more. Would you run an errand for me? I've just thought of a way that we can keep track of him without having to stay so dangerously close."

After agreeing and getting her instructions, she rode down the trail at full speed. Tyler couldn't help but admire her 'muscle tone' while she rode away from him.

Kendra took the car as directed, found the pocket fisherman, reeled it in, and grabbed the pack. She went to the liquor store on St. Armand's Circle, which had opened at eight o'clock sharp as usual, and rode back to meet Tyler at the tree.

She watched with curiosity as Tyler emptied the pack and slit its lining, then slid the FM transmitter and another device into the gap between the lining and the canvas outer layer.

"This is a miniature GPS transmitter, accurate to within three meters," he whispered, "and the gadget from the fishing pole is a wireless mic. If we leave the pack on the beach for him to take, we can monitor his calls - AND his exact location - without having to be so close."

With one of the towels from the pack, he made a bundle of most of the other stuff, then re-loaded one towel, his spare shirt, shorts and - most importantly - the cold six-pack of beer, into the pack. "Come on - let's go swimming now and distract him."

While walking down the beach towards where Tony was fuming, Tyler yelled "Whooo-hooo, MILLER TIME," as loud as he could and made a show of pulling a beer from the pack before he waded into the shallow water of the bay. Then he splashed around some while pretending to drink the beer. But most of it was poured into the bay each time he lowered the can.

Kendra yelled, followed him, and dove right in. When she came out she shook her head like a dog and water flew off her short blonde hair. Tyler got a face full, and in 'retaliation' splashed her with a double handful of water.

He playfully shoved her in the direction of the bikes. She got the idea, and they wrestled their way further and further from Tony and the knapsack. After much splashing and pushing and yelling, Tyler pulled Kendra tightly up against himself and really laid one on her. He felt her melt into the kiss and admitted to himself that it sure was as nice as a kiss could be.

They held the comfortable pose for a convincing time. He grabbed her hand after finally breaking the embrace and they waded up to land. Hand in hand, they strolled back along the beach away from Tony, then into the woods near the tree, sans knapsack.

It would have seemed obvious to most anyone where they were headed to do what, and even Tony was not too slow to pick up the clue. He casually strolled up to the pack as they watched from hiding - idly picked it up, did an about face, and ambled back to his bench.

Stifling an exclamation of triumph, Tyler turned on the radio, donned one earbud, and gave the other to Kendra. They could clearly hear the cans banging against each other as the pack was carried. Then a thump. Then rummaging. A sudden shout made them wince in pain, "ICE COLD!" There was a POP sound and much gurgling.

They silently stole away back to the car and home base, soaking wet. Each was glad to be breaking the sweat and chilling in the breeze, while riding through the cool, shade covered trail.

Chapter 06

Kathy Anne Hines, AKA Susan Kane / Erika Lucci / Erika Kane / Susan Lucci, was born in 1957 in Talladega, Alabama. She was the only daughter of a used car salesman/wannabe stock car racer and a regular homemaker - the revered occupation of all women in her time and place. The family lived in an old mill house with a dirt drive and a dirt yard and several ex-cars in the yard. The family was as Baptist as they could be; which Kathy/Erika/Susan countered by being as irreverent as she could be.

Shortly after turning sixteen, she came home drunk late one night, announced her pregnancy by a local mechanic who was way into his twenties, went to bed despite her father's tirade and her mother's tears, and took off in the wee hours in her father's pickup truck (the one that ran).

The pregnancy was aborted in New Orleans by virtue of her mother's butter-and-egg money, which Kathy had helped herself to when she left. She sold the pickup to a gas station attendant - without any paperwork - for a hundred dollars, then ran off to Hollywood to become a world famous actress, and is still running. Most of her acting was, unfortunately, done on her back, or else spinning around a fire pole in the flashing lights of a strip club.

Susan took off in her shiny, white Sebring convertible after her first conversation with Tony; holding a cigarette in her right hand, with her left hand poised to show her 'emotional finger' to anyone who looked at her wrong - or right, for that matter. She always dealt with anger and emotions by driving around aimlessly. She was custom made for the streets of Sarasota, Florida.

Knowing Tony to be on Lido, she headed for Siesta Key, the next island south, and went straight to the Daiquiri Deck to get decked on daiquiris, a breakfast ritual she often practiced after lining her nose with expensive powder. Food was never a part of this ritual, since she had to keep her waist wasped for when the 'Big Break' came.

After two entrees she decided to walk on the beach in the late morning sun. She had dressed formally, so she removed her full wrap to reveal Victoria's Secrets in their bright red splendor. They were rather flimsy, but she always thought it fun to show off the results of the major tucking operation that Tony had paid for.

Since a full nose plus alcohol plus no food plus bright sun always made her a tad bit dizzy, she ended the walk early. Turning around to return to the car she ran headlong into her large octogenarian retinue, scattering the guys just like so many well dried bones. She jiggled her way back to the car just as Tony made his fourth call to her.

This was a close emotional encounter for them, as much as either could manage. She yelled, and he stayed quiet. He yelled, and she cried. Finally, she broke down and agreed to come rescue her "poor boy", especially since she knew he had some money, and knew her stash was getting light. Actually, between shouting sessions, it became nonexistent just before she drove away, deciding in her heavy buzz to not rewrap the wrap.

With the top down, creeping through the rush hour traffic in Siesta Village, she caused quite a stir, or caused quite a few to stir, as the case may be.

Driving like this was her release, and nearly that of many a male passerby, as well. She was in her element, and passing through town to change islands, became more and more convinced that she was off to save her knight. Susan was often confused by reality, those times that she encountered and recognized it.

Rushton Woodside

Chapter 07

Tony drank two of the beers in rapid succession, and began to return to his own nature, though oblivious to the beauty of the nature around him. He knew it would take most of the beers to brace himself for Susan. She was obviously in one of those moods - the ones caused by running out of nose candy. If she were to hurry up and get him before she went too far down, they could go to the mainland and score, then pack up and try another town.

He explored the knapsack further and found Tyler's clothes, then ducked into the woods and changed into the rather tight fitting outfit. He buried his bloody clothes in the loose sand in a clearing. This left a problem: there was no way to pack the gun in Tyler's shorts without showing it as obviously as Susan showed her assets. After wrapping the gun in the towel, Tony traded it for a third beer, and spent nearly two minutes enjoying that one. He was feeling better and better. His previously flattened ego began to recover.

A check of his wallet produced sixty dollars, which was not near enough to satisfy his partner's needs. But checking all the pouches on the backpack proved to his benefit. Another almost-hundred plus the almost-hundred he had was, well, over a hundred. Tony never excelled at math, except for counting drinks up to four, which he did now, and found that he was left with one more beer, which was already warm from the sub tropical heat.

Twenty minutes had passed since he and Susan had made their arrangements, so he started to head back towards the parking lot, leaving four cans strewn about by the bench and holding the last, which he sipped as he walked, the nearly empty backpack slung over one shoulder.

Just as he thought what beautiful smells nature had he reached a picnic table set back in the shade from the beach. His homeless buddies were there, toking up on a big fat joint.

"Hey," he hollered, "I thought I smelled something good. You guys gonna share some?"

"Hell yeah, if you got some more butts for us. We found a little patch of this dank growing deep in the jungle here in the park. It's a little moist still, but stays lit."

They went about trading smokes and tokes, and Tony was soon feeling ready to take on the world, and even Susan. "Man, I'd buy some o' dis from ya if ya'd lemme."

"Well, we need beer money and cig money and you seem cool," said the obvious leader, the one with most of his teeth. "Gimme forty bucks and I'll split it with you."

"Deal! See, I gotta face my ol' lady soon, she's comin' here, and a buzz on me makes her into somebody I can talk to pretty good." Nobody got the joke, especially Tony.

Money changed hands, and one of the lesser evils took off on a rusted old bike to get supplies with one of the twenties. That left Tony and two Streets to burn some more. They talked a while about history, which means: 'who stole more, beat up more people in worse ways, and what a piece of crap the government is'.

They were trying to figure out who the current president of the United States was, when Tony's cellphone rang, startling his two new friends.

"Hey babes. Talk to me."

"Tony, I'm in the parking lot you sent me to. You better come on now, so we can get outta here."

"Lissen babes, I'm just down da beach to the left, an' got some treats goin' on down here. Take a walk. Strut yer stuff. I know ya like to show it, so show it on down here."

Susan was too excited at the word 'treats' to argue, though she didn't know that he had the wrong kind. She couldn't tell how fried Tony was, since he existed outside her world, which consisted of her bountiful body and her little brain. She and Victoria's accessories got out of the car and strutted off to the left. The Mennonite women turned away at the sight while their husbands pretended to.

Tyler and Kendra had set up at a picnic table of their own, with his laptop online through his cellphone - setup to monitor the GPS signal - and the shared earbuds from the radio. They had watched Tony move and re-settle, listened to the dealing going on, watched the biker heading towards the store, and heard Tony's side of the conversation with Susan.

It wasn't difficult for them to figure out who was strutting which stuff when Susan went past them. Kendra even placed a restraining hand on Tyler's thigh due to a fit of temporary jealousy. She then guardedly changed the grab to a series of pats as she explained that she was going to go get the license number of the car.

Susan picked up the predictable following from the picnic area, including a couple of Mennonite teenagers who wandered onto the beach with their heads stuck sideways as her bouncy parts jiggled along and barely stayed within Victoria's constraints.

Tony's voice came through the earbuds, following a good old-fashioned wolf whistle.

"Babes. Yer slipping. Dere's only four guys walkin' behind ya. I wancha ta meet Deke and Zeke here. Zack went off to da store fer stuff. Har!"

"Hey, boys" she said to the two slack faces. "Where's the treats?"

"Right here babes," said Tony, offering a joint. "Best I've had in months. Da boys here grew it in da woods dere!" He pointed away from the beach.

"That's for kids like you, Tone. Where's my stuff?"

"Soons we get off the island, we'll getcha some."

"I wasted a good strut and there's no rut?" she complained, grabbing him by the shirtfront and shaking him. "You mean I gave this show for free? I can do that when I want to, but not for you, Buddy!"

He knew the keyword 'Buddy' too well. When combined with a shirt grab it meant real trouble. She began shaking him harder then - teeth clenched -

nose beginning to run - and he was reminded of the time in Galveston, when he had to walk funny for a couple of weeks after she was done with him.

He subconsciously changed his stance so that his legs were closer together as a flash of the previous night's adrenaline started to flow back into his body. She had him cornered, and he was nervous, and was real high by then, becoming highly paranoid.

"Sorry, babes, just kiddin'. I gotchya rut here, in this bag I found. It was fulla money, too. It's just like last night really happened, after all. I got all ya need right here."

Deke and Zeke had just started to back away a bit as he reached into the bag. They didn't like the way this was going down all of a sudden. There was too much anger. Before they knew it, he'd pulled out a little gun, a Dick Tracy special, and held it close in to the front of his stomach, pointed it right at the foxy lady.

Tony was so tired and high that he wavered side to side as Susan jerked him forward and back again and again.

The 'boys' yelled and took off running. Zeke bounced off a palm tree, recovered and then actually passed Deke as they hit the edge of the woods and disappeared, without a sound.

Susan shook Tony continually, but shook him one time too many, one time too hard. The gun fired solely from the motion.

Tyler and Kendra heard the shot through the earbuds, and were on their feet before the actual noise hit their ears by the normal route. They stood frozen as the echoes died away, and heard Tony yell "SHIT", and Susan moan. There were loud shuffling sounds.

Tyler looked down just in time to see the icon on the GPS screen flash and skip away from the beach with each blink. They heard nothing as they yanked out their earbuds and ran as fast as they could down the beach. Tyler slowed enough to call 911 on his cell phone, then babbled to the operator as he picked up the pace again.

Kendra reached Susan first, a heap on the sand, now wearing red in one extra spot, right in her midriff. She watched them arrive with bleary eyes.

"Bastard didn't give me any!" she yelled, and pointed towards where Tony had gone. She fought off the initial attempt at being helped up, screamed: "Have you got the rut? Did he send you here with it? I'm ready now!"

Kendra wasn't quite sure what the woman was talking about, but having seen her previous display, made a correct assumption and then an apparently soothing answer.

"It's coming soon, honey. There'll be enough for everybody. You can have all you want."

She stripped off the tank top which she wore over her bikini, and gently pressed it against Susan's entry wound as she spoke, hoping that there was enough 'rut' in the girl's system to keep the pain down some.

"Let me help you up to the table, you must have fallen down. Your 'rut' will be here soon. We can have some here at the table, okay?"

An awkward minute later, Susan was stretched across Kendra's lap on the bench seat, arms draped over stomach to hold the rapidly darkening cotton. Susan's eyes were clamped shut. She actually did seem unaware of what had happened.

Tyler caught up finally, having been forced to stop running to get past the babbling and breathlessness to explain to the operator what was going on. He took in the situation. He had seen the woman point, and he leaned in that direction and looked at Kendra briefly before he took off running himself.

At first there were skewed footprints in the loose sand to follow, and then an obvious trail, part of the park. The pine straw showed a pattern akin to the footprints, so he continued, and reached a little wooden footbridge over a canal. This spurred an unconscious memory of his having heard the rubber-mallet-on-boat noise again in the distance as he had dialed his phone moments before.

Over the bridge the trail made a hard right, which he knew led it right back to the beach. To the left, mangrove swamps. He chose the swamps, moved slowly so as to remain alert for any sign of recent passage, torn clothing, whatever.

Nothing seemed obvious, and he had to stop. There were no trails. One could zigzag between the scattered trees and middens in random patterns. Then he heard a splash, way off, but the direction from which it came was easy for him to calculate.

It was too late in the morning and too hot for it to be an animal, so he figured it was Tony. WAIT! Tony had a gun! But . . . who could shoot in this swamp? The chances of a direct line of sight were very slim, since there was so much undergrowth.

His pent-up anger overruled his fear. He was the highly experienced woodsman pitted against the yachtsman, the city boy. He calmed himself.

A silent mantra - a memory from the sixties. Listening, listening intently. Moving again, stalking towards the fading noise, stalking silently, eyes wide, nostrils flaring. Deeper into the swamp, no more sound of the breaking surf. Insects buzzing. He had to fight off a flashback: jungle tried to replace swamp in his mind, his hands subconsciously moved to where they would be were he cradling his M16 at ready, but when he started to brush away some vines with his bayonet he shook that memory away and snapped back to the present. To Tony.

He knew he was getting close to the origin of the splash, and slowed even more, finally saw an unnatural wet spot ahead past a tidal pool, froze where he was, scanned like a machine. Eyes. Nostrils. Ears. Finally, one single spot yards ahead called for his attention.

A tiny trampled mangrove shoot. Tyler took a deep breath, moved farther, deeper in, his sweat ran everywhere. He stepped cautiously up onto a midden and spotted a definite wrong color through the trees ahead, and dropped to a crouch. There was no movement, no sound. The color, though out of place, seemed familiar. Damn! The backpack.

A siren wailed in the distance, a real one - not electronic. Of course: it was the fire engine that always accompanies an ambulance. The station was a scant mile away on the north end of the key. His eternity in the jungle had been a minute in the swamp.

The distant sound of a helicopter at full bore gave him more information. Tony would have heard that, too, and then dug in. The authorities had all day to close in on him.

Tyler shook his head, wiped his sweaty brow with his forearm, and headed back to the scene, of the shooting, memorized his path as he went back. There were more sirens, real modern ones. All of a sudden he knew he was in for a very long morning, and would probably have to explain the events of the day under pressure. He decided that he was a fool to not have called the police in the very beginning.

Chapter 08

Kendra Christina Jorgensen was born in 1964 in Zurich, and was handed life on many golden platters. Her stepfather (Johan Straub, son of a renounced German) was the owner of a bank that was confidential in nature, and her mother came from minor Hungarian royalty by way of Sweden and her first husband. Private tutors gave her enough information in her first sixteen years to educate several people. Travel accounted for over half of each of these years. She had access to the family's vacation homes in Lisbon, Monaco, Palermo, and St. Moritz (her favorite) and where she spent as much time as possible.

At eighteen, she was still a virgin and was married off to an older (much older) maternal cousin with stars in her eyes. At the no-longer-ripe age of nineteen, she became a divorce' with Johan's blessings, and a bank account that she was told had no ceiling. She decided to do some real traveling and find the right place to settle down.

Disgruntled after a few months in New York, a year and a half in Venice Beach, and three years in a high rise in South Beach, she went to Sarasota to check out the Ringling School of Art, where she eventually received several degrees and became an instructor in Renaissance Studies. She religiously teaches three afternoons a week, nine months a year, and has her salary deposited directly into the bank account of a local charity, the Safe Place and Rape Crisis Center. She also works in their SPARCC Treasure Chest store on Saturdays year round.

She bought a cozy fourteen-room Spanish Revival mansion on Lido Key from a world-renowned anthropologist. Kendra was familiar with the house from pictures that her grandfather had taken during an extended trip to the United States, when he was an up and coming factor in the banking industry.

He was visiting the Van Wezels, diamond merchants from Antwerp, who had built and still owned the home. Grandpa Straub got their account, the biggest coup of his career, which then allowed him to simply open his own bank, using their deposits. To his delight, and Kendra's eventual benefit, many other people worldwide wished to bank where the Van Wezels banked.

The house had not been officially for sale when Kendra moved to Sarasota, but she made an offer so generous that the law of the land took precedent. Everything in Sarasota is for sale.

She has longed with all her heart to share the home with her friend of three years, Tyler Polk, and has offered him the house, the indoor pool, the docks replete with several boats, and the bank account, on a regular basis.

She never really had the chance to be a kid when she was a child, never played board games or spin the bottle or doctor. With Susan in her lap, though, Kendra finally had a chance to play nurse, and ran the situation quite well.

Tyler was somewhere near calm when he returned to find Kendra still comforting the injured woman, and looking daggers at him.

A diesel engine idled in the background and there were some subdued shouts in several different voices. He realized his phone was lying in the sand only when it rang, and he remembered that the last thing the operator had told him was to stay on the line so that the medics could locate them.

He answered sheepishly: "I'm sorry, ma'am. There was too much going on. I'll find your people right now. OH SHIT!"

The phone hit the sand again as two uniformed policemen appeared, running down the beach with guns drawn, and he shot both of his hands straight up into the air.

"FREEZE!" he was told. Freeze he did, until he was motioned off to the side by either Mr. Smith or Mr. Wesson, held firmly in two very competent looking hands. The small group of on-looking beach-goers all eagerly hit the water.

The other policeman (Wesson or Smith) talked to his shoulder mic calmly, turned to face the direction of the parking area, and waved his hands in the air. Medics were followed by firefighters, who were followed by even more Smiths and Wessons. They all made a rather strange sight in their ragged Conga line as they struggled to run in the loose sand with their heavy shoes and boots on. They converged on the picnic table, the two women, and the apparent suspect whose wavering hands would have kept away the largest of mosquitoes.

One officer motioned Tyler towards the trunk of a large Australian pine and told him to assume the position. He didn't know the phrase, but watched COPS very occasionally on TV without the sound, and knew what was expected. He did a real good job of assuming the position.

A swarm of various types of uniforms formed around the two women as Tyler was frisked and told to sit in the sand. Kerplunk to the sand he went, and he tried to make his voice work, to tell them that he was the one who had called them there. He managed some croaking noises that were puny against the officer's string of questions.

A different officer came over, placed his hand on the first's shoulder, and became Good Cop, dropped to one knee with: "Are you the gentleman who called?"

"Yesss - Yes! I had been following this strange man like I told your operator and then I heard a shot and then ran down here while calling 911 and I found she'd been hurt and my friend stayed with her while I tried to chase the man but he lost me in the jungle, I mean the swamp, but he dropped my backpack so we can't use the GPS to track him anymore, but I know what he's wearing 'cause it's my other clothes and if you cordon off the preserve he won't get away anywhere 'cause the girl with the bullet is his ride to safety from where he shot the guy that wouldn't give him money for the pictures of the hurt girl who's not his wife."

Once Tyler stopped to breathe, the two uniforms looked at each other. Smith told Wesson that it was obvious to him who was on first, then laughed, looked at Tyler, and explained that a tech would be there soon to check him for powder residue.

Susan heard that comment, and managed a moan: "Bring the powder - bring the powder." The cops looked at each other again. One nodded slowly.

The other said that the every time he had to respond to a gunshot on Lido there was 'powder' involved.

Two of the larger firefighters helped to load Susan onto one of the wheeled gurneys they use, and awkwardly hauled her down the beach. She had a death grip on Kendra, who had no choice but to follow. A plainclothesman tried his best to talk to both of them; tried to take notes as he stumbled along the beach with the whole entourage. Finally, one of the medics waved him away, and in frustration he headed Tyler's way.

Obviously not the good cop, he barked: "What the hell is going on here? Why did you shoot that woman? Was this a puny attempt at a rape, beach boy?"

Tyler's only response sounded something like "Garggghhh." He was shaking fitfully by then, glancing at each of the three men in turn, over and over.

Smith took over. "Lieutenant, we don't think this is the perp, and from what we can tell he was actually trying to help out here. He did more than gargle when we first spoke to him, though not much more. Apparently, he had followed an unknown perp who shot the woman, and then tried to chase him down after the incident. We verified a nine-one-one from his cellphone. He told us that there's a backpack that belonged to the real perp out in the woods."

This sudden act of random kindness on the officer's part stirred Tyler into some semblance of reality.

"Yes, Lieutenant, he's right. All this started when I was fishing before dawn this morning."

"Yes, Mr. ..."

"Polk. Tyler Polk. I'm a resident of the key. "

"Please go on, Mr. Polk. Or may I just call you Tyler?"

"Yes sir, you may."

Tyler went on to relate most of the morning's events to the suddenly pleasant plainclothesman. It took quite a while. As the events all were laid out, the plainclothesman's eyes got wider and wider.

He finally spoke: "Tyler, just what made you think you were qualified, or justified, or within your rights, to stalk this Tony you're talking about. You obviously could have gotten shot yourself!"

"Sir! It wasn't stalking. I didn't think you guys would listen to me with what little I knew. I didn't know he had a gun, thought he might have been a victim himself." Tyler's head dropped. "I'm sorry, sir. It just seemed the right thing to do, is all."

"Stand up Tyler. I'm Lieutenant Shake. Our techs are going to be delayed a while. Please hold out your hands, palm up, so I can see if you've fired a weapon yourself."

Tyler passed the crude sniff test, feeling as if he was making a new dog friend in the process. Shake asked him to show them the backpack.

Chapter 09

It was a mean looking squad that strolled off into the depths of the park. One officer led, his sidearm held in both hands, but pointed at the ground. Tyler gave directions from several yards back, walking beside Shake, and the other officer took up the rear. It was a surprise to Tyler how little distance he had traveled during the chase.

They retrieved the pack and were back to the scene in maybe five minutes, where Shake emptied it onto the table. There wasn't much to find. He had Tyler repeat the whole story from start to finish.

The chopper had begun a slow spiraling process very close to the ground. Two more officers arrived with eager dogs straining at their leads. Both dogs went crazy immediately, found a clump of the marijuana flowers beside the picnic table, and obviously thought their workday was through. The officers gave them the "Track" command, though, and they clocked back in. After circling the table once they went straight for the woods, noses scrabbling the ground.

Tyler had to explain his way out of all new trouble with the pot they had found. Shake was head on with him staring at his eyes, and seemed convinced, though. Then he asked to see Susan's car. Tyler obliged, his ID was returned, and he was dismissed with a warning to remain accessible.

Since Kendra had accompanied Susan in the ambulance, he morosely loaded everything back into his car, not even cognizant of the fact that his laptop had been left out to be stolen and wasn't. He was about to get in and crawl back home when a hand on his shoulder claimed his very last dregs of adrenaline.

"Tyler, is this the gentleman involved?" queried the lieutenant, gesturing at a bedraggled and handcuffed Zeke. "Your description was so vague that we're checking anybody the dogs find."

"No sir. I guess he's the drug dealer."

"We figured that part out, Sherlock. Martin, just book him on the class 'A' he was carrying. Tyler, call us if you remember anything else, Okay? Go get some rest. You look like hell."

"Feel like hell, sir. Will do. Thank you."

As Tyler drove, he made the first of many frustrating calls to Kendra's cell phone. They continued as he unloaded, as he hosed off the bikes, as he finally stretched his lanky frame out on the aluminum lounge chair that was permanently bolted to his dock in the beginning of the afternoon shade. He tried to take a nap, to get some rest.

Each and every call caused a vibration in Kendra's pocket: in the ambulance, in the waiting area, and in pre-op. She ignored them all until the IV took hold and Susan's hand finally relaxed. She ran to the bathroom, and finally called him back.

Tyler greeted her with a sleepy "Hurro."

"Darling, are you OK? They didn't arrest you?"

"No, just chastised me for being the fool I am but keep forgetting about. Have they been bothering you?"

"They've left me alone. I've been glued to the poor hurt woman until just now. I did hear the police officer that was guarding us talk to someone on his little radio, and telling them that he could come over to question me soon."

"That'd be Shake. He's a detective. He'll be nice. He must believe me since I'm at home now. I explained to him how you were just with me at the very end. Did the woman tell you anything? Oh, are you at Sarasota Memorial?"

"Yes and yes. But I just want to stay out of this, Tyler. I'm not even going to tell you what she said. It was girl stuff. Your Tony's not very nice."

"You did the right thing Ken, going with her like that. I'll come wait in the lobby. Call me when you're done with the lieutenant. We'll walk over to Hillview and have a stiff drink or three. And he's not MY Tony."

"Tyler, I'm sorry, I know he's not. I'll see you soon, okay? Bring me a hug."

Sighing deeply, Tyler replied simply: "Of course. See you soon ..."

He drove to the hospital immediately after he took a long cold shower, and then waited for what seemed like hours in the main lobby.

Chapter 10

Lido Key has very special sunsets, since it is surrounded by water, and only a few hundred yards wide. Face any direction and you get a great one. The Gulf side sunsets are fantastic, of course, especially if there is a green flash.

If one's view is towards the bay, towards the city, the sunset can often be better than the view over the gulf. The clouds will pick up the colors being refracted off of the water. Orange, magenta, deep purple, all etched with streaks of gray that represent the lower altitudes, the clouds and wisps that are below the direct line of the final rays of sunlight.

Once this happens, looking away from the sun, one can see the first of the stars, the ones that shine so brightly in the clean island air. If the moon is rising, as it was that night, if it is full, as it was that night, it grows hazy rings.

Tony didn't give a damn. To him, the greatest moments of his day had been when the sound of the chopper faded away, when the dogs were called in from their steady search thirty feet below, and especially when one of the voices on the static-laden radios had called to "pull it in, boys" just as dusk came in.

He was one large muscle cramp from all of the exertion of the long day, now propped up against the trunk of a mangrove tree, as high as he had been able to climb. No jungle training from the military had been on his side, nor had any Boy Scout time, just a random piece of luck.

While running at his very limit, he had meant to leap across one of the myriad canals in the park. His long stride had just placed one foot on the top of a midden, and he launched from that step, only to fly into the arms of the tree.

It had hurt like hell, pinpricks of pain all over the front of his body. Having unbuttoned Tyler's tropical shirt to strut for Zeke and crew, the tree had left him looking like a worn out pincushion. It had also left him up in the air. He scrambled further up, until the branches were starting to sag under his weight, then he kept climbing until the canal was just a black shimmer flickering below him, barely visible through the thick leaves.

Once stopped, he wedged himself into place, and spent a long time dabbing repeatedly at spots of fresh blood with the tail of the shirt. Over and over, bleed - dab - sting; bleed - dab - sting.

When the dogs had stopped at his last footprint and started whining and sniffing around, their handlers made the obvious assumption, that he had gone into the canal and had waded away in the water to kill his trail. They went one way, and then another. They split up, went past the canal, and occasionally returned to that last trace of his trail.

Nobody had ever looked up. The tree was too far from that last footprint. They had not imagined him flying through the air to his overgrown hideout. He had always thought the mangroves were ugly trees, but this one had made him see the beauty of the tangled limbs.

Luck was literally in the wind, too. There was a ten-knot onshore breeze. The dogs kept expressing interest in an area way downwind, but the tangle of the branches of the myriad trees in the swamp was dispersing Tony's scent so much that they could never home in on him.

He had not heard sirens leaving, but the sound of a real V8 engine in perfect performance tune was easy to pick up on. One by one, the cruisers left the park. He knew it would be stupid to think they had all left. Whether they thought he had left the key or not, there would still be at least one squad car left behind.

As far as he knew, he had now killed two people within a few hours of each other, and the police could probably associate him with the second one. Just like his lack of time in the military, his lack of time behind bars was very important to him. He finally shifted enough to retrieve the thirty-eight from his hip pocket. Bullets weren't beers. He hadn't been counting. A check of the cylinder showed only one left.

Tony had never shot anyone before, but might have to again, and the thought that he had only one chance worried him. Cops usually come in pairs, and you can't shoot two with one bullet.

Next, he dug his and Tyler's cash out of a pocket and counted slowly, methodically. He had a total of a hundred and twenty dollars left. That could get him somewhere if he had a chance to get to the bus depot.

After the last of the colors faded from the sky, the full moon took over, and he decided to move again. He clambered down the tree as silently as he could and squished onto the marshland. Strange noises were all about him, and he felt sure that the one snake he had seen during the day had relatives, and being a city boy, he wasn't quite sure what else might hang around in the woods at night.

The moon was in the east. He knew he wanted north, and zigzagged off through the tangled thickets with the moon on his right. It wasn't long before lights became evident through the trees and traffic noises became louder. He found a well-maintained trail that made it easy to reach the edge of the park. There were motels and condos across the street. He found a convenient tree to climb into and waited for the right time to go on.

Time dragged. Laughter came from one of the motels (a party in progress), people walked their silly little dogs, fewer and fewer cars went by (though every third or fourth was a patrol car), the moon got higher.

Finally Tony stepped nonchalantly onto the sidewalk, and headed across the main street towards the beach in search of an unlocked car, some fresh clothes, a new image. He didn't know he was being watched.

Rushton Woodside

Chapter 11

About three pm, Tyler met Kendra after the lieutenant was done with the interview. The couple walked in silence to a club near the hospital, holding hands. Things were slow that time of day, so they had privacy to talk once they were seated at an outside table, sipping drinks.

He started: "How's Susan?"

"She seems okay. She didn't let go of me until the pain killers kicked in, so I was able to hear what the ER nurses were saying. The wound looked messy, but apparently due to the angle of the trajectory the bullet passed through without hitting anything major."

"Bet she'll be ticked off if there's a scar."

"Ha, I'll bet she'll be wondering why there is a scar."

"That far out of it, huh?"

"Yes. I'd explained to the medics in the ambulance that she had seemed to be pretty high when we first saw her, so they did a blood test. The ER doctor and his nurse were arguing over how much or how little pain-killer to give her, if any! "

"So how're you holding up, Kendra? Did Shake give you a hard time?"

"No. He was very nice. Asked for a brief summary of what I'd seen. He made notes and nodded, and seemed satisfied. Asked for a description of your buddy, but I really couldn't help him much with that. He told me to stay available should he have any more questions, got both my phone numbers, asked me to call if I happened to remember any more details."

"Same for me . . . . ."

"Darling, tell me you're through with this, okay?"

"I'm through. Lesson learned. Shake reamed me pretty intently about not calling them first. He said that if there is a body somewhere, they don't know about it yet, and that I ruined their chance at a head start."

"Hey, let's finish these drinks and go home. The whole day is catching up with me. I need to lie down."

They drove in silence back to Lido. Tyler went in with Kendra, got her settled in the living room. Beethoven helped her relax, and before long she was asleep. Tyler went down to her dock, watched the day wane. Tried to forget about Tony, to no avail. He went back in after a while, and she was still sleeping heavily. He restarted the CD, put it on repeat, and left a note saying he was going to go ride to clear his head.

Back at the dockhouse he got out his road bike - the one with two self-contained electric wheels (thanks again, Sharper Image) - and switched his phone to vibrate. A trip to the park showed what he expected, two patrol cars, each at a different end of the parking lot. He assumed that they hadn't found Tony yet.

Tyler continued to pedal for the exercise, and went to the north end of the park, where he had first seen Tony from the bushes, then proceeded to ride around the closest block repeatedly. Nobody paid him any attention. Idle cruising was part of the island life.

Around he went: South Boulevard of the Presidents to Roosevelt to Ben Franklin to Taft. Trip after trip. When the sun was almost down completely, he saw a familiar colored pattern, highlighted by the moon, at the edge of the woods in a tree out of the corner of his eye. He almost passed it by, but after a second glance back over his shoulder, he knew. His Shirt!

He rode to the end of Roosevelt, stopped, and watched. He waited a long time. Finally, the shirt appeared, headed towards the beach. He should have called Shake, he knew, but he didn't.

Tony had caused him and Kendra a lot of grief, and he wanted to be involved. Shake would just send him home, and besides, by the time he got there, Tony would be gone. So Tyler walked about a block behind on the opposite side of the street, bike alongside. He noticed how obvious the gun was in the pocket of the ill-fitting shorts.

Tony seemed right at home, not hurrying, not dawdling. He was a man out having his evening constitutional, by all appearances. He turned into the Lido Pavilion parking lot, and headed towards the back, away from the street.

He thought back to his teenage years, lifting stuff from unlocked cars, how he had gotten the thirty-eight he so treasured, and tried every car in the back row with a quick yank on each door.

Finally the back door of a minivan opened for him. He glanced around and hopped in, then emerged quickly in new clothes, a loose T-shirt with some garish logo on it and a red baseball cap, but still wearing the same shorts.

Tyler watched from behind a clump of sea grapes as Tony walked out onto the beach, and then walked the bike over and out in slow pursuit. Tony had gone up to the edge of the shore and sat down, watching the final colors of the almost endless Sarasota sunset. With the help of the moon, Tyler was able to go a considerable distance past and settle in himself, a gray blur on the beach, just able to see the sitting hulk.

Finally he saw motion, standing, walking. Tony walked right past twenty feet in front of Tyler, ambling down the edge of the water. The nearness made Tyler shudder, but he gathered himself up and followed.

They went back up to Ben Franklin, past the condos, right through St. Armand's Circle, all the restaurant smells making Tyler remember that he hadn't eaten all day. But he pressed on anyway. Once they had made it to the causeway towards the mainland he was able to lay back. He knew that Tony was unlikely to jump a wall to one of the mansions lining the causeway. The only places to stop were the two bridges that went over the bay.

As Tony reached the second one, the new monstrous fixed span, Tyler cut in his motors and went right past him on the broad sidewalk. The bay air at fifteen miles per hour cooled him and relaxed him considerably.

Once over the bridge, he pulled underneath, where the bait shop was on a little access road, drank heartily of the water he had been hoarding, and waited. Eventually, they were a pair again, both bearing right at Tamiami Trail, down the sidewalks of Bayfront Park. Tyler pedaled slowly in second gear, saved his batteries.

At the edge of Sarasota Bay, there is an area where sailboats are moored year round. Dinghies and dories - and a clan of homeless persons - use the beach as a gathering spot. Those lucky enough to have bikes chained them to nearby trees. It was well known that they parked there and slept in the woods bordering Marie Selby Botanical Gardens.

The Gardens staff included security which patrolled the paved paths at night, but that wasn't where the people camped. They stayed close to the bay, mingled in with the mangroves, essentially invisible. The police knew that this happened, but figured that isolated homeless were better than scattered homeless, so let it go on. This was where Tony finally stopped walking. With his new garb he fit right in. In his rumpled shorts, docksiders that now looked worn out, wrinkled T-shirt and ratty ball cap he looked just like he too shopped at the Salvation Army.

Tyler settled on a bench between streetlights so he could see without being seen, watched and waited. He saw Tony wave something in the air, hand something to two different men. The men took off in two different directions on bicycles, and Tony settled in on a sun-bleached log with the rest of the ragtag crew. One man rode past Tyler on the jogging path, and returned within a couple of minutes with two brown paper bags in the front basket of his rattletrap bike. Beers were passed around, tops popped, and cigarettes lit. The other guy came back and everyone huddled together on the log.

Soon, the pungent smell of a burning joint wafted through the air, and reminded Tyler of Viet Nam again, especially under those circumstances, staked out and watching the "enemy". He could hear deep coughing and the crowd grew boisterous and loud enough to hear.

"Damn good shit!" in Tony's voice.
"Hell yeah. Tol' ya it'd be."
"Roll it all up. We'll smoke it all!"
"Hell, yeah, let's do it,"
"Hey, this beer won't last long. Go again."

Another trip to Main Street brought back two more bags. They all got rowdy as could be, and finally started slumping, falling over if they tried to stand up, peeing right into the bay. A couple of them stumbled into the woods on a path Tyler hadn't noticed before, then another man in a different direction. That left two guys, Tony, and one untidy woman, who had been clinging to him more and more as the night went on.

The last of the men went into the woods, leaving the lovebirds on the log all by themselves. They lurched into a fumbling embrace. Tyler saw a shirt raised up and off, saw flesh, another shirt, more flesh, marveled at how this was all happening twenty feet off of US Highway 41, down on a small beach outside the sea wall.

The woman giggled like her mystery date had turned out to be Pierce Brosnan. She wasn't used to guys that could buy beers for everybody, especially twice in one night! Tony was grunting like a Neanderthal. He started to push her down on the sand, but she resisted, led him down the trail instead.

Inspiration struck Tyler: sneak after them, find the sure to be discarded shorts, scarf the gun, head back to the well lit park, and call Shake. Tell him he had seen Tony while on a random ride in the park, and not mention the following part this time. Nobody else would get shot. Tony would be arrested. All would be well.

Chapter 12

Lieutenant Shake, born Michael Garner Shake in 1948 in Pittsburgh, was the son of a policeman and an ER nurse. He was imbedded with the goal of growing up to be yet another person who helps those in trouble.

He lived an entirely uneventful childhood with one exception. His parents - in fine Irish fashion - called him Mick. There was no Seymour Butts in Pittsburgh, but there was a "Mick Shake". His childhood was a nightmare of stupid jokes, there not being much else to do in those days.

His girlfriend in high school was much in the same boat, being Clara Belle English. It seemed that almost everyone who had not watched Howdy Doody at least once was able to come up with 'Cow Bell' as a nickname for her, and the remaining few just

just thought her name was funny of its own sake. Mick called her Cutie, because that she was. They dated through their junior and senior years, and married after he enlisted in the Army.

In 1966, when he hit boot camp eager to go help Lyndon and Hubert fight the Commies, he found great delight in being constantly referred to as simply 'Shake', so never went by Mick again.

Now when he answers the phone, it always sounds like he's commanding a dog to perform, even if he answers from a dead sleep.

After Kendra called the station with a problem, and dispatch then called him at home, he gave his usual business bark.

"Shake!" A look at the clock: ten twelve p.m.

"Lieutenant, one of the people you interviewed about the shooting on Lido just called. Something about her friend being missing, she said he's been kidnapped. She didn't make a lot of sense."

"What's her number?"

He down the number, but got up and went out onto his lanai so as to not disturb Cutie, who had mumbled in her sleep 'not again, honey'. He wasn't sure if she meant the phone call, or was dreaming that he wanted to go a second round that night, a rarity for them.

"Hello" Kendra said in a shaky voice, after answering during the first ring.

"Ms. Jorgensen, this is Lieutenant Shake here. I understand that you called the station."

"Thank you for calling back so soon. I'm not sure where to begin. Mr. Polk had brought me home from the hospital. I laid down for some rest and went to sleep. When I woke up after a long nap, he was gone. Well, he lives right down the street, so I walked down to clear my head after the nap, and perhaps to get a little comfort from him, but he wasn't home. One of his bicycles was gone. He didn't answer his cell phone."

"Yes, when was this?" Shake prompted, to keep her going, keep her from breaking down.

"A couple of hours ago. I searched the key, knowing all of his favorite spots to meditate, then went back to his place. He still wasn't home."

Geez, meditate, thought Shake.

"I called his phone repeatedly," her voice got weak again, "and finally a stranger answered. It sounded an awful lot like the guy that Tyler was following today."

Shake could tell she was about to cry, and talked to talk, repeating what she had just said: "The voice was the same as you heard over the spy mike this morning?"

"Yes sir." (Sounding like 'Sa-hir'.)

"He said that he had Tyler, and wanted money before he would release him. Ten thousand dollars."

Full sobbing stopped the conversation for a long minute. Shake waited patiently.

Finally: "The money's not a problem, Officer Shake, I can get it in the morning. I'm just worried that this lunatic is going to hurt Tyler."

Shake put on his best grieving widow voice: "Ms. Jorgensen, just stay calm. I have worked many such situations in the past. If we just cooperate with the man we can get your boyfriend back. Did the man give a meeting place and time?"

She said that she was supposed to call Tony at eleven the next morning, and explained that she was expected to make a money drop at the marina in Bayfront Park at noon, at which point Tyler would be released. After ascertaining that she was all right by herself, Shake arranged to meet her at her house at ten am, told her that they would save her friend and the money, no problem.

Kendra spent a sleepless night on her couch, while Shake was back to sleep in five minutes flat. Up at seven as usual. Breakfast on the lanai at eight. As he was finishing his breakfast, and talking on his landline to the station about the plans for high noon, his cell rang. He saw Dispatch on the caller id. He told the sergeant: "Hangon" - one word - stabbed a button and barked again: "Shake!"

It was a call he had been half expecting since the morning before. A housekeeper had entered her employer's residence on Otter Key. One sprawled body, lots of blood. Cars were en-route, and Shake was had been given the investigation.

He acknowledged, went back to his first call, explained to the sergeant briefly, and left Cutie with a peck on the cheek and the usual dishes.

He strolled to the driveway and hopped into his city assigned car, which had been confiscated from some local yuppies cum convicts who thought that Sarasota would be the ideal spot to avoid port authorities with a large load of South American snow. They had bragged too much and one lost his house to the state. The other lost his 1972 Malibu SS. His loss was Shake's gain. He added to the collection of tire burns on the street in front of his house. Cutie watched, slowly shaking her head, thinking 'Boys and their toys.'

He drove with the traffic, which was much faster than if he had put his bubble up and hit the siren. That just slowed everybody down. In a small town like Sarasota, all the patrolmen knew his car, metal-flake blue with the twin white stripes, so he knew he had clear sailing. Commuters hugged his rear bumper, enjoying the pace.

A doctor in a BMW Z3 nearly lost it as the Malibu ate up the hairpin turn at the bay and zoomed by, passing within twenty yards of the bench where Tyler Polk had spent his late night hours. One of Tony's new friends had to dive for the median as Shake conspicuously ran a red light at the causeway. Over the big bridge and left onto the key, he arrived in less than ten minutes, minus the two gallons of gas used during the six-mile ride from home. City gas - paid by taxes.

One radio had arrived, and the tape was up, blocking the drive. Shake always felt out of place during his rare calls to these estates. This time a two story Greek revival mansion awaited him, with full colonnade. He thought it to be damned ugly, a pink box surrounded by fluted columns that looked just like cell bars in the city jail. Two stone lions flanked the front steps, posed as if to scare away the common people. Past them, within the colonnade, the officer at the scene comforted a Mennonite woman, apparently the maid. The patrolman nodded towards the open front door.

Shake did a Don Johnson with his sunglasses and walked in. Marble floors and dark furniture in the entryway, one wall lit up from the skylight, a dome unbelievably far above.

He saw a discarded broom down a hallway to his left, entered the adjacent room. He saw one well-dressed man lying on the floor, his right hand stretched towards the door with all fingers extended. 'The Death Wave.'

Otherwise the corpse was fairly fetal, and the blood was mostly dried, only a few spots indicating a slight sheen.

Noticing a table lamp laying askew on the floor, with the side facing up shattered, Shake knew that there would be a bullet somewhere in the room. Finding the stray would be much easier than waiting for the coroner to dig one out for him. A full scan of the room showed one painting swung out, one wall safe - unopened. Nothing else looked out of the ordinary.

Shake closed his eyes, dropped his head as if in prayer, and backed out, remembering not to touch the door, leaving it ajar.

The crime scene techs wouldn't be far behind him. Though there was only the pair employed by the city, they had work on just a few days a month in the normally sleepy city and would have already been at the station, taking their eternal coffee break.

Whoever did this was certain to not be in the house, and would have to have been Tony, who was apparently busy with Tyler Polk at the moment. Shake went and waited with the patrolman and the housekeeper, eye contact the only conversation until she stopped crying.

Shake broke the silence: "Ma'am, is there someone we can call for you? Someone you need here now?"

"Yes sir. Call Elijah, please, sir." She rattled off a telephone number.

He called and explained, offered to send a car to pick the man up. Got his address. Using the radio, he arranged for transportation.

"He's on the way, Ms........." (head cocked in his friendliest expression).

"Yoder, sir. Mary Lee, call me Mary Lee. Everyone does, there are too many Yoders here in town. Why Mr. Petrosky, sir? What would he have done? Was he in trouble?"

Pleased that she was now talking, Shake slowly shook his head. "Not that I'm aware of. All we know so far, Mary Lee, is what you know and what we've seen. Since you're alone, I assume that there is no family at home now." Keeping away from actual questions, not wanting to exert any pressure on the woman.

"Yes sir - I mean - No sir. The Mrs. is out of town again, off to Bermuda again, I think. Their children are all grown up and still living in New York. All of the grandchildren are still with them, some in college, some not quite yet out of the Academy."

Nodding: "Sounds like you've worked for the Petroskys for some time, Mary Lee."

"Yes sir. Seven years. Ever since they retired and moved here. He retired, I mean. The Mrs. never worked that I know of. She is a fine lady, what will we tell her?"

84

He was pleased with her detachment, very fast recovery. The Mennonites are very strong people, emotionally as well as physically.

"The police department will take care of that, Mary Lee. We just want to make sure that you're okay first. Then hopefully you can help us out by letting us know how to contact her. I see that our medical team is arriving. Will you excuse me, please? The officer will stay with you until Elijah arrives, which should be soon."

"Yes sir."

Shake nodded politely, then walked halfway down the drive to meet the techs, not as a courtesy, just to get away from Mary Lee's eyes. Those who found death always scared him, probably due to his just not having any idea what it was like to be personally involved. He always came later. Never knew the bodies as people. Working a homicide has to be like that. A body. Not a person. Never lived. Never talked. An object. Cold because it was never warm. A job has to be fun, and if it's not fun, it still can't be depressing or overwhelming.

"Johnson & Johnson! How are you guys?" (His standard greeting for David Miller and Joan Headley - had to put humor where there was none).

Joan always did the talking, and used her standard opening: "Wha's shakin'? I see bereaved.

Is the party inside?" (Trying to keep it light. Has to be fun or you can't sleep at night, can't look at the mortality of your own loved ones).

Shake simply nodded and led the way. Happy hour was over and it was time to be tight-lipped and serious. They could tell from the look in his eyes and his expression that an ugly mess awaited them inside.

He stood in the hallway as they worked. Death confirmed. Digital photos. Chalk lines. A bullet found in the corner, tweezed up into a zip-lock. They started methodically dusting every surface for prints

"Thirty-eight?" asked Shake.

Joan said: "Looks like it. You already got this one solved, Shaky? Is this tied in with the one at the park yesterday? The runway model we heard about?"

"Could be... there was a Dudley Do-Right on the scene who said that he had overheard the perp talking about something that'll most likely turn out to be this mess. We found a thirty-eight slug in the sand with the metal detector. Had to dig three feet down to get it. The girl wasn't wearing enough to slow it down much. Not much body fat either. Looked like she usually ate through her nose." He closed one nostril with his index finger and sniffed. "A witness described a nickel plate being wielded at the victim."

"Sounds like you're on a roll, no shaky puddin' this time. Got any leads on this guy's whereabouts?"

"That's the next act. Perp has Dudley in hand and has asked for some spending money. Guess that safe was never opened."

"Ouch," complained Joan, "Triple ouch in our little paradise. I know the press has act one covered. ABC7 was live this morning at the park. Pointed at the picnic table, showed the blood stains dried in the sand. Woman's still at Sarasota Memorial. They have wind of this yet, or your other little situation?"

"They'll have this off their scanner. Probably outside now. The part with Dudley is stricto confidentialo, okay?"

"Mum's the word, Shaker. We're done here. I'll stay to handle the coroner. David can dust his way outside. You off to handle act three now?"

"Yep. Thanks, guys. Lemme know what happens when you work the match between yesterday's slug and that one."

Back outside, reality was the usual shock. Elijah was there, as were at least a dozen uniforms. Shake took a moment to explain to the Yoders that a gunpowder residue test was required on Mary Lee. They perked up, glad to help in any way. He shouldered off the press that had gathered at the tape with a "No comment", quietly cranked the Malibu, and eased off the clutch in second gear. He kept all the rubber on the tires this time out of respect, and putted back to the causeway.

It was nine thirty. He had time to grab a coffee at the Circle Diner before meeting Ms. Jorgensen. Time to stop at the beach, breathe the salt air, change heads.

Chapter 13

The head of the trail proved easy to find, but after that it had been faint and difficult to follow in the dark. Branches scratched Tyler and he nearly tripped twice on roots. He froze each time to listen for movement in the brush. He was not being very stealthy at all. His drill sergeant from 1970, Jack Woods (nicknamed Yak), would have been really mad, would have waved his service revolver in Tyler's face, saying: "Bang you're dead, Boy! Bang you're dead!"

Tony and the woman made enough noise coupling to cover his stumbling sounds, though, and he navigated his way towards the sound. Closer and closer. He finally saw his own yellow shorts lying in a heap on the sand, the lovers a few feet away but oblivious to the outside world. He crouched down, felt the gun in a pocket, and was about to pull it out, then pull himself out.

"Gotchya, Summbitch!" was the last thing he heard before his head exploded in pain and he went out like the proverbial light. The homeless have one main creed, which is that "Nobody should steal from somebody else before I get a chance to", and that was what had gotten Tyler.

Eventually, he heard the lovely musical tinkle of halyards slapping masts in the morning wind. With his eyes still closed, and him shivering in the humid breeze, it was as if he had anchored in the bay among the sailboats by the marina, and was waiting to have breakfast downtown after a night fishing run. He thought he felt his boat rocking gently, thought that he had wedged himself down between the seats to sleep, that once again his arms had gone numb from that awkward position, and that the heavy salt air was making breathing difficult.

He didn't know the rocking sensation was from the mild concussion that he received from an aluminum baseball bat, that he was wedged between mangrove roots, that his arms were numb from being tied behind him and around the tree's trunk, and that his breathing was impaired by being gagged with his own shirt.

Opening his eyes hurt so much that he closed them back immediately, reminded of hangovers from his youth.

He felt throbbing instead of rocking now. His torso was cramped and his arms hurt. He noticed the gag and said: "Mmmmmphh."

Nobody answered. Opening his eyes slowly brought nothing but confusion until he remembered "Gotchya, Summbitch" and the pain, and where he must be. He tried "Mmmmmphh" again, and heard a woman's raspy voice.

"Hey, beach boy's awake." (Why was he Beach Boy all of a sudden, no matter where he went?)

A too familiar voice replied: "Cool. Hey bud, you're buying us breakfast. Jay pulled da cash outta yer wallet after he caught ya trying to nab my stash, ya sleazebag. He'll be back from McDonald's soon. Hope ya don't mind watching us eat."

"Mmmmmphh."

"Hey - yer girlfriend can feed ya after she pays us to getcher scrawny ass back."

"MMMMMMPHH!!!"

"How much? Is dat what you said? Ten g's. Shoulda asked for more, but hey - no sense in being greedy. Didn't go after ya in da first place. Has she got dat much handy, dat Kindra? I sure am glad dat she called right after Jay knocked yer lights out.

Your phone didn't ring, but flashed her name just after I picked it up, so I answered. What I don't understand is why ya was here in da woods, all done up in yer fancy duds, diggin' for my stash. Ya know dese folks livin' here are honest folks. Don't like stealing. Dey're just all down on their luck, like me right now. Hey - here comes da food!"

Tyler's vision was becoming normal again, and he didn't like what he saw. The woman was riffling through his wallet, and held up each credit card in turn, staring at the holograms cross-eyed. She looked right at home in the woods, sun-dried, wrinkled and dirty.

Tony had the gun wedged in his belt. Someone who must have been Jay tromped down the trail with his arms full of McGarbage bags, and several other people appeared in the clearing and gathered around as he handed out breakfast sandwiches. Like hungry animals, they all turned their backs on each other as they ate, hunched over their food. There was actual grunting going on. Tyler closed his eyes and waited. Far from hungry, he began to wonder what it would be like to throw up when gagged. He tried a pleading: "Mmmph?" (Meaning "Would you please take this gag off of me so I can breathe?").

Tony stared at him, said: "Listen Bud, I tol' ya your chick'd feed ya. If ya don't shuddup I'll have Jay put ya back to sleep."

"Hey, Big Tony, lemme do it again. That was some sound when the bat connected. Who'd a thought they'd make a bat outta metal? I'm sure glad I found this thing floating in the bay."

"Jay, jus' wait. Mebbe he'll be quiet." Tony looked at Tyler's phone. "We need him ta be able ta walk in a coupla hours. Ya wanna walk don't ya, Mr. Polk?"

Tyler chose a silent nod for his answer, sighed, closed his eyes again, and listened to the people eat. His other senses were coming back now that he had sight under control. He could smell the inviting smell of the greasy food, the salt air, the wonderful aromas coming from the gardens, and - unfortunately - the stench of human urine, which, as he thought about it, began to dominate. He figured it was too far to walk to the park's public bathrooms every beer or so, over and over again.

It was hard for him to judge the time of day from the subdued light that filtered through the virtual rain forest, which grew to the bay from Selby Gardens. He became aware of the traffic noise after he heard a really hot big block GM screech through the hairpin turn and then roar north towards downtown. This gave him some idea that it was rush hour - such as Sarasota has. Nothing gave him any idea what to do about his situation. If he even had a league, he would be way out of it.

A jab to his shoulder brought his eyes wide open. Jay prodded him in the shoulder with the dreaded baseball bat.

"Hey, buddy, wanted to ask you something. Your fancy electric bike that was chained to the light pole up there by the cement path, the one that I unlocked with your keys here, is it got a lot of electricity in it? Seems like it sorta slowed down when I brought the food back, but that coulda been the wind."

"Mmmph."

"Well, I gotta tell you, Mr. Poke, it's the coolest thing I ever rode. I've had a lotta Harleys in my day, and I like that bike as much!" He pushed harder into Tyler's shoulder with the bat on gotta and coolest and rode and Harleys and lotta, and really hard on much.

Tyler was bored with his current vocabulary and just stared up at the man, nodded his head, raised his eyebrows, shrugged.

"JAY - leave da man alone," said Tony, "we got business brewing here, and I don't give a rat's ass about no automatic bike. We gotta plan where to meet his chick wit the money. I don't really know where we are and where's a good spot, so les talk about that insteada some crummy bike. I betcha never even rode a Harley anyway."

"Sorry Big Tony. I did though, well sorta. My older bro' owned one, and so did Skeeter and Tree. They all lemme ride 'em. I stole my bro's three wheeler to get here to Florida, yes I did."

"Mmmph." (Which meant: Please do not bring Kendra into this, I can get you ten thousand dollars right away if we just walk down to Sarasota Bank, and I just don't give a damn about your motorcycle days.)

"You shuddup too, Polk. Yer woman's gonna call us once she's got the cash, and we'll trade ya to her. Then ya can talk some real words, not this 'Mmmm' crap."

One more "Mmmph" brought the bat down on his shin, and Jay leaned real close, face-to-face. "Big T sed to shuddup, Poke."

Tyler nodded. Tony pulled Jay upright and put his arm around his shoulder. They walked off down the trail, apparently on their way to discuss the exchange in private. They talked animatedly for a while, just visible through the trees. Jay finally pointed out into the bay, towards the sailboats at anchor. Tony nodded slowly, a big smile on his face. When they came back, he was still smiling.

"Mr. Polk, I'd liketa take dat gag offa ya, cause yer chicky friend should be calling us soon.

I'm gonna wancha to talk to her, tell her yer okay, not to bring any cops, just da money. But, if I do letcha talk, ya gotta promise to stay quiet until I hand ya da phone. No yellin' fer help. Okay?"

"Mm-" Tyler stopped himself as the bat was swung back in a bowling pose. While imagining an upper cut to the chin with the bat, he nodded.

Tony looked at the woman, leaned his head towards Tyler, and said: "Jeannie, go take da shirt outta his mouth. Don't keep it."

She got up to obey, and as she got closer, Tyler realized that he had never known how bad a person could smell, could reek of sweat, alcohol, urine, and worse. He had the strange thought that Tony would probably suffer pretty badly soon for his night of joy in her arms, and inside her body, which had to be much worse than the outside. After tossing his shirt in his lap, she kneeled down beside him and put her hand on his thigh.

"Tony, I wanna keep him, he's so pretty." She moved her hand enough to make Tyler very nervous.

"Dammit, Jeannie, he's worth money. Besides, ain't I enough for ya? Now get yer hand outta his crotch."

She glared at Tony, stood up, and returned to his side. Tyler finally began the breathing he'd been scared to do when she was close. Deep breaths, mouth open, his heart raced. Tony's gun showed in his pocket, and Jay idly swatted at the underbrush with the bat. All the others had faded into the woods after they ate, but those two were enough to cause him to worry about whether or not Kendra would receive him alive and unbroken.

The gang sat down. Tony fired up a joint, and the three of them passed it around, and followed it with one last warm beer that Jay had pulled out from between some mangrove roots. Jeannie kept casting sidelong glances at Tyler, a twinkle in her obviously permanent bloodshot eyes. He was grateful for the rank smell of the reefer, it was far better than the general environment, and he felt that he might have been getting a slight buzz from the second hand smoke.

It was just enough to relax him a little bit and relieve his growing collection of aches and pains, just enough to make him have to stifle a laugh when he thought again of how Tony would probably pay for his free sex. The next time Jeannie glanced his way, Tyler actually smiled at her.

After the joint was done, the two guys got comfortable. Jeannie passed out. Tyler was thirsty and hungry, and he nodded into and out of consciousness.

Eventually, the buzz of his phone vibrating woke everyone up. Apparently, woods dwellers must be light sleepers to be able to stay alive, unharmed, and in possession of whatever worldly goods they might have to call their own.

Chapter 14

Shake decided to not tell Kendra about his morning, part one. She had no need to know right then, though the media would take care of that soon enough. There was enough on her mind right now without knowing how hardball the kidnapper was, without knowing that he had actually murdered someone.

Watching the mailboxes on South Boulevard of the Presidents on Lido Key, Shake looked for five thirty five, and tried to remember why that number seemed familiar. It wasn't something that he had written down as part of a crime scene. He had a funny memory for details like that.

When the right mailbox appeared he was shocked. That was the one home that nobody was familiar with. There is no house associated with the street address, just a wall of dense tropical foliage, which started on a six-foot high dirt berm that ran along the edge of the road at the property line and would keep the house fairly safe from most storm surges that could build in the shallow Gulf waters.

He remembered a case in 1994, involving a shooting on the north end of the key, when he had cruised the key all day and all night, watching for a certain blue van. He tracked the progress of a hippie yardman who had built the berm out of sand dredged from the median of the boulevard, shaped it with merely a shovel. He had worked all throughout the heat of the day. Over the next few months, he occasionally saw the same old hippie plant all sorts of exotics on the edge of the property. Even before that project had been started, there was no house visible. Now it was literally as dark as the Amazon beyond the roadway.

Shake remembered judging it to be about a five acre estate, enough for eight - maybe ten - of the Miami inspired mansions that had sprung up along the boulevard since Hurricane Andrew hit Miami in the early nineties. It seemed obvious that Kendra Jorgensen had access to ten thousand dollars.

There were several shell driveways that led into the property. He chose the one adjacent to the mailbox, and entered a virtual tunnel of pink oleander that curved enough so that he could no longer see the road in his rear view mirror. The shell was fresh and crunched under his tires. He parked next to an incredibly well preserved red XKE sedan and walked to the only building he saw, which appeared to have originally been a carriage house many years ago.

The same hippie (someone Shake now realized worked at a local bookshop) answered his knock, and directed him towards one of the many paths that left the driveway at random angles. Shake decided to save the marijuana smell that emanated from the caretaker's quarters for another day's work, and followed the man's directions.

The designated path led Shake to a gate which had a sign which read 'For Dog's sake, please keep gate closed', and then went underneath the branches of a pair of neatly trimmed Queen palms, which made a smaller tunnel effect than he had experienced when he drove into the estate.

It was almost ten o'clock in the morning, but Shake felt cool as he walked down the path, as if the property were air-conditioned. Once past the palms, he stopped, stared at the sixty-foot tall king and coconut palms in the yard. There was a century plant in bloom on his left, an oyster plant clump large as a van on his right. He saw many bromeliads scattered around, and wild orchids and tiger lilies drew circles on a mound where the path split and rejoined. Frangipanis of all colors were abundant. The caretaker obviously did good work.

His eyes finally settled on the rambling Spanish house, done in mission style, tile roof and lots of wrought iron. The smell of chlorine from a swimming pool, barely discernible amidst the intoxicating perfumes of all the tropicals, brought him back to the mission at hand. He followed the path to a double wide red door, decided that the brass gong was the doorbell, and patted it gently with the wooden mallet that hung on a chain, waited. Kendra swung the door open. She looked to be in bad shape.

"Thank you for coming, officer. I have never had to call the police for anything before, and never thought I would," she said as she led him into the depths of the house. "Coffee? I have some fresh, and iced, as well."

She led him to a room at the rear of the house. It had a view of both the pool and the main canal that cut between Lido and Otter Keys.

"Yes, ma'am, if you don't mind. Iced and black would be great. Have you gathered the money? We'll try to keep it or get it right back to you."

He expected her to ring for a maid, or several, but she stepped into the adjacent kitchen and answered over a stool lined counter top.

"Oh yes, what was not laying around the house was easily accessible through the teller machine. I really do not care about the money, just about Tyler's safety." She returned with his drink and indicated a chair for him, sat opposite.

He ignored the 'laying around' comment, and went into his calm-the-victim mode. "Ma'am, I have every belief that we can get Mr. Polk back home safely." The memory of Petrosky's body flashed through his mind as he said this.

The standard grill followed: Tyler's height, weight, hair and eye color; did she know what he had been wearing; describe the bike that was gone; had the man given any clues about the meeting; was there any background noise during the phone conversation?

Kendra stood up pretty well through this. Most people in her situation would break up at each question, Shake knew; yet she remained calm, looked him in the eyes, and thought through each answer, especially the last. She seemed to struggle, eyebrows drawn down, and then finally answered.

"Well, I could tell the man was outside. The cicadas were quite loud, and there was wind blowing through trees, and across the mouthpiece of Tyler's phone. And there was an unusual noise. Sort of a loud humming, almost. It changed tones, seemed to slow and get lower. And ... something else. I heard what might have been a party in the background, laughter - very faint - tropical music, too, steel drums, now that I think about it. Yes! There was a cocktail party in the background, but the humming noise, too. I don't understand the humming, even though it now seems so familiar to me, something so familiar." She drew her face tight after this last comment, obviously trying to recall the conversation in it's every detail.

Shake busily took notes, and used his intermittent polite nod as he wrote. He almost looked like one of the little plastic birds you buy at tourist attractions, the ones that bob into a glass of water over and over. Once she began to struggle with the familiarity of the noise, though, he froze. He knew not to disturb someone performing mental recall of important facts. His hand stayed poised over the notepad.

As they both remained paused, a humming noise started to intrude on his thoughts as well, as if he too were right there with her, in her memory. It was a sound that he also knew was familiar, something he should be able to name right away.

He glanced away from her, didn't want to disturb her state of concentration. Looked out into the canal, saw a palm tree moving in the wind. No, a palm tree was moving towards him, over the tops of the palms in the yard. He smiled suddenly, knew the answer, and waited for her to notice and identify the source.

Her eyes got wide. She spoke - slowly.

"It's as if I hear it now, but getting louder instead of fainter. It's just like ..."

She jumped up and looked southward down the canal. There was a tremendous houseboat type of craft with potted palms on the top deck and tourists who took pictures of the mansion.

"Just like LeBarge! The party boat that comes through the canal every morning! I heard LeBarge in the background, with the sounds of the band and the evening sunset party! Does that help? It was about nine-thirty. Can you find out where the boat was then, Officer Shake?"

"Yes, ma'am, I can." (He still ignored being called officer; she was too upset to be corrected over something trivial like that.)

He called the station on his cell, and got someone going on the lead right away, holding for the answer, looking at her with the silly face that people use when put on hold while someone is watching, the raised eyebrows, head going tick-tock, back and forth, like one of those cat clocks on the wall from the sixties, the ones that have become popular again. Finally he came alert, nodded once, thanked someone, asked to be transferred to dispatch.

"Hey, Terry, Shake here. Working an MP case. Seems to be turning into a ransomed kidnap. Need some cover at Bayfront Park, phasing in slowly and building up until noon, which is payoff time. As many plain as you can get. No bubbles, bicycles if possible. Staggered arrivals, cover the whole park, but pay special attention to 'South Beach', where the rummies sneak into Selby at night. Any of them leave; we want to know where they go. Tell any uniforms that might be there now to leave as soon as the plains start arriving. We want no profile on this. Also, a general BOLO on one white electric bicycle, motors on both hubs, saddlebag batteries, headlight. Need to know if any patrols have seen the bike since, oh, about eight p.m. last night. Call me back if you get anything at all on the bike or it's current whereabouts."

He clicked the call off, and returned his attention to Kendra, though still watching LeBarge out of the corner of his eye as the oblivious tourists partied their way down the canal, enjoying their glimpse of paradise, of the mansions.

"Ms. Jorgensen, I've been told that at about nine-thirty LeBarge was just pulling into her dock, with, as you heard, a large party aboard. This Tony that you two had been stalking yesterday had made friends with some bums on Lido, and I'll bet he's done the same again near the bayfront. Do you think Mr. Polk might have been stalking this man again?"

"He as much as promised me he wouldn't. But ... he didn't exactly promise. He's pretty headstrong once he gets something on his mind. Maybe he did... that's the only reason I could give for his disappearance."

Shake smirked and nodded his head. He reminded her that it was almost time to call, asked if there were two telephones close to each other so he could both be with her and listen in when she called. She suggested they go to her office and use the speakerphone. He agreed. They did.

She called promptly at eleven as instructed. Shake had a digital recorder pointed at the speaker on the phone.

Tony saw her name on the caller ID and answered gruffly. Nothing but "Got da money, girlie?"

"Yes. Yes sir, I do."

"Jus' lissen to me, den. Put it in a bag, like a grocery bag or something. Go to da park on da bay downtown, where dere's a walkin' path goes round in circles, on a little island, like. Walk until ya hear one of us call yer name, Kindra. Got it?"

"Yes sir."

"Now lissen up good. Dis ain't playin' round. We got guns. If I see anybody looks like a cop, we're jus' gonna shoot yer Mr. Polk and then leave him somewheres. Dey can find him sometime. Do ya unnerstand? I'm gonna let ya talk to him, now. He can tellya we got guns, we ain't jus' messin' wit ya. OK? Den talk to me again."

"Please - put him on the telephone," she whimpered.

Tyler's voice soothed her ears when he said: "Kendra, It's me. These guys are serious. Just do as they say, and do not call the police into this. Do exactly what they say. Do not call the police."

"I will darling. There are no policemen with me right now," she said, and looked at the single policeman.

He understood what she meant. Of course she had the police involved, she would have to be scared to death. Tony had seemed like an amateur at this so far. Things would probably go well.

"Goodbye, Kendra. I'll see you soon."

"Goodbye, darling."

Tony came back on the line and asked her to wear something really unique so they could spot her easily. She told him that she would wear an orange shirt, orange hat, and lime green shorts.

The connection went dead, and Shake replayed the recording that he had made, then called the direct line to dispatch once more, confirmed a kidnap, the twelve o'clock meeting at the park and explained that the buyer would be strolling the jogger's walk on Island Park. He described what she would be wearing, and asked for as many plains as could be gotten, even if duty cops had to change clothes and ride the bus to get to the scene.

Kendra went to the back of the house to change, and by the time she was done it was time to go. Shake confirmed that no less than thirty officers and detectives would be onsite, scattered across the mile long stretch of park. His instructions to her were simple: walk around the path as instructed, hold the bag tightly, and don't worry about her safety. They headed off in separate cars.

As he drove behind her, he wished that all the buyers he had dealt with in the past were as calm as she had been through the process. He hoped that she stayed that way until the capture.

Rushton Woodside

Chapter 15

Having grown up in Detroit, Jay had always found enjoyment in watching boats and boaters.

He continued that hobby in Sarasota, and watched the bay religiously each day. He knew the schedules of many of the sailors who kept their boats at anchor there. One sailor, in particular, had a daily routine that involved inflating a small Zodiac, which he brought to the waterfront in his car, attaching an outboard, and leaving the rig at his mooring while out sailing. Jay had pointed the Zodiac out to Tony when they went aside in the woods, and explained that it would be a breeze to steal it and take 'Poke' over to one of the sailboats moored close to the park.

Jay never really learned to swim, so once the shallow bottom dropped off too much to wade, he did a sort of dog paddle the rest of the way to the mooring, and found that he was more scared of the water than he had previously thought. After the swim, and boarding the boat along with an awful lot of water, he did just as he had seen the sailor do every week, and actually managed to start the engine on the third pull. It was twenty minutes before noon. He successfully guided the boat over to the shoreline and picked up Tony and Tyler. Jeannie raised a fit at being told there wasn't enough room for her.

They cruised over to a cluster of sailboats which were moored fairly close to the jogging path on Island Park, and Tony climbed onto the vacant two-masted schooner, the 'Sea Before', after getting Tyler aboard, which wasn't easy considering that his hands were still bound with an old piece of rope.

Meanwhile, one of the other denizens of the woods, Sonny, walked over to the park, headed around the path, and settled on a bench close to the Sea Before. The bench was at an angle so he could see people as they came down the path, which was nearly deserted this time of day due to the late spring heat.

There was only a scattering of people in the park, a couple of them sat at picnic tables reading, a man fishing a little ways down the shore; there was one lone jogger. They were all police officers. Jay had pulled onto the beach a few yards from the bench and was busily bailing out the seawater, which he hadn't anticipated, with an empty plastic jug that came with the Zodiac. Tony and Tyler lay low in the cabin of the Sea Before, at the cost of one broken teak hatch. Tony peered out a porthole, watched his perfect plan take place.

Shake was one of the apparent lunchtime readers. He sat on a table at the top of a little rise in the center of the park. He had a suspicious eye on Sonny, but paid no attention to Jay. He recognized several of the bystanders as being from the force. He admired his perfect plan taking place.

He knew that if the man on the bench was involved, it would be an easy pick; he could easily be coerced into revealing where Mr. Polk was hidden.

Kendra soon rounded the bend at the north end of the island and headed towards Sonny, a Publix grocery bag clutched tightly to her side. As she neared, he leaned forward with hand extended, palm up, as if asking for a handout.

Tony saw her orange clothing, pushed Tyler out onto the rear deck, and had him stand up. Jay finished bailing, climbed aboard and cranked up the outboard.

Sonny said, "Look out there, Miss. Your friend is on that big sailboat. Now hop in the rubber boat real fast, and you'll be taken to him."

She did as she was told. Jay backed out like a pro, turned ninety degrees against the shore, switched gears and gunned the engine, a big smile on his face. He glanced back casually and to his surprise saw people running his way - fast - holding guns, and a man on the hill yelling into a radio.

Two men converged on Sonny's bench. Other men and women hit the water on foot behind the Zodiac. Jay turned his attention back to where he was going, and saw that while his head was turned, Kendra had gotten up from between the seats where the thrust had dumped her, and was reaching for the gas line that went to the tank between his feet. He kicked at her ineffectually.

The boat swerved drastically (not his intention), which threw her back down. They were closing on the Sea Before rapidly, but Jay figured the swimmers wouldn't be far behind. He heard a gunshot ring out behind him. There was no sign of Tony or Tyler.

Jay did some quick math, such as he could, and figured a blonde with a bag of money was a hell of a lot better than people with guns. He roughly changed course and headed out into the main body of Sarasota Bay, passing close enough to the sailboat to cause it to rock immediately from his wake. He caught a snatch of Tony's voice as he passed.

"MOTHERFU..."

There was a flurry of gunshots behind him, so he ducked down as far as he could and still be able to navigate. His marine experience was limited to one fishing trip on the Myakka River at Snook Haven a few years back, which made his path a little ragged while trying to steer from a squat. To his advantage, none of the bullets hit the rubber sides of the Zodiac. He went to the right, passed under the big bridge, and didn't slow down in the no-wake zone.

Tony stayed down on the deck, holding Tyler's neck from the front with a strong grip, the gun pressed against his left temple. The boat stopped rocking. He heard all of the shots - returning none - and lots of splashing and yelling. He wasn't able to hear what Shake yelled into his radio, but did hear the distinct beep that comes from police radios, and the authoritative voice which followed.

"Dispatch! Shake here! Where's the damn patrol boat? Get it to bay front now! No! To the bridge, north side of the Ringling. The kidnappers used a boat to get away with the buyer and the payoff. Get the chopper up. We're looking for a little yellow Zodiac hauling ass north."

He clicked off, pissed off. He had simply not expected this turn. It was his screw up, and sleep would come with bad nightmares once he found he could sleep again, which would only be after this was all resolved. He called his forces in, and stared at the ground, wishing for a rock to kick.

Tony waited, staring at his watch, at the second hand sweeping around and around, but not paying attention to the minute hand. He didn't loosen his grip on either throat or gun. There was a nice onshore breeze that he ignored. There were no other sounds.

After a while, he eased his left hand back, and then pulled the gun around in front of himself, keeping it trained right at Tyler's head. He crept backwards on his knees, making enough space to stop any lunge that might be made towards him, and slowly raised his head enough to see over the gunwale. A quick peek showed that there was a small crowd of people, and that two uniformed policemen were talking to Sonny, who sported a pair of handcuffs behind his back. Tony jerked his head back down to wait some more, starting to breathe easier. Jay had screwed him over big time, but apparently the police didn't know that he and Tyler were onboard the sailboat.

Meanwhile, Kendra had backed into the bow of the little boat to wedge herself into a safe position while the maniac beach bum tried to drive. He was getting no safety awards that day. They had turned left after passing under the bridge, and were barreling through the crowd of wind surfers that always populated that area. Those that could still stand after the boat passed waved angry fists as they clung to their masts.

Jay reached the shallows, and the ride got smoother. He slowed a bit, and turned to go under the smaller bridge on the causeway. The water was like glass on the other side, being closed in by two of John Ringling's man-made islands, and he opened the throttle completely. They soared away on a plane at thirty knots, all the craft would do.

Rushton Woodside

Chapter 16

Susan opened her eyes to blinding whiteness, and then clamped them shut and cried out weakly.

"Hello ... Hello! Is anybody there? It's breakfast time. Where's the rut?"

She had no idea where she was, where she'd been, or what had happened the day before. That was not an overly unusual state for her to be in, but what was strange was that she couldn't move her arm to wipe her runny nose, the nose that always told her when it was time for more Coke.

With a whopper of a hangover, more like from the days when she was into downers in California than from a night's worth of drinking, she knew she needed a line really bad, knew that would perk her right up.

Trying to roll over on her side to start the process of getting out of bed without making her head explode, she found that her left arm wouldn't tuck under her ribs, and that her right wouldn't follow the roll of her body. Then she realized what was going on. She and Tony must have been playing games again the night before, games with the rope that she had soaked in fabric softener all day right after they met. She liked those games, liked the rope, the blindfolds, the mysterious and unseen foreign objects.

"Tony, honey. Let me up, now. Are we already done? You can move the light away from my eyes now, I've confessed. I'm a bad girl."

Her voice seemed to be coming from somewhere else, or from somebody else. It was very slow and groggy sounding to her.

"Tony. Dammit! You have to let me up RIGHT NOW!" she screamed using that other person's voice.

It echoed strangely. Using all her breath like that sent a stream of pain shooting through her stomach as it stressed the bullet wound. She got scared and was worried that he had gone too far this time. Using skills she had honed over the years, she opened her eyes a tiny crack, held them there for most of a minute, and then opened them a little more. Bit by bit the hospital room came into focus.

Then it all came flooding back to her. The beach. Tony being an ass. The drug tease. The gunshot. The pretty lady with the soft hand. The ambulance.

She focused enough to see the call button resting on the edge of the bed, hit it repeatedly. A drive-through speaker voice sounded over her head.

"Miss, what seems to be the problem?"

"This whole thing is a problem, dammit. Get your butt in here and talk to me. Untie me from this bed."

A haughty answer: "Someone will be in there as soon as possible, Miss."

When the nurse entered the room a few minutes later, she told Susan that she would have to straighten back up to avoid tearing her stitches, and asked her how much pain she was experiencing.

"My stomach hurts way bad, but I'm jonesing worse. I bet you don't give out coke here, but you gotta give me something."

"Ms. Kane, you're due for medication soon. I'll be right back with some pills for you. Your cousin wanted us to call her when you woke up. Are you ready for me to do that now?"

"My what? Oh, you mean the lady who came with me. Sure, please call her; maybe she can help me out. You bring me some kind of pills first, though, anything you can. Get these plastic things off my arms too, would you?"

After explaining that the restraints were there by virtue of the police, not the hospital, the nurse ignored Susan's ranting and raving, and went back to her station and made two calls before getting the woman some Demerol.

The first call was to security, to have them contact the police and inform them that Susan was awake, and the second was to Kendra's cell phone, which began vibrating unheeded against her hip in the speeding Zodiac, just as she was passing underneath the Ringling Causeway in a runaway rubber boat.

Chapter 17

Tyler had become dazed from thirst, and was confused by whatever had just happened. After all of the activity, after he had heard the Mariner nine-point-five cruising past them at full throttle with gunshots sounding across the water, after Tony had yelled out one more humongous cussword, he had been shoved back into the hot cabin of the sailboat, which was only being ventilated through the open hatchway. All of the portholes were still sealed and the air was simply stifling.

The general concept seemed to be that the exchange had not worked out. That much seemed obvious from the gunshots and yelling, and the fact that he had heard the Zodiac speed by. His only hope lay in the fact that he could hear a helicopter .

He was worried about Kendra. He knew that if things had gone correctly, he would be in her arms right now, or at the very least out of Tony's control. As long as the gun was pointed in his direction, he felt it best to not ask any questions, though. The man looked very pissed off about what had taken place.

For a long time very little happened. The helicopter got further and further away, audibly circling its way over the bay. Tyler lay still on a bench seat, sweating profusely. Tony sat at the little galley table, gun in hand, occasionally turning to peek out of a starboard porthole. His other hand was occupied with a liter bottle of Jack Daniels that he had found in one of the cabinets. He finally found his rhythm as the hard liquor kicked in. Round and round he went. Stare at Tyler, take a swig, and peer out the porthole. Stare, swallow, peek. Finally he spoke.

"Mr. Polk. Guess ya know things got screwed up here. Yer girlfriend brought da cops wit her. She met wit Jay like we planned, but da cops was right behind 'em. Jay took off in da little boat, just kept goin on past us. He's got my money. Now, whattaya think I outta do wit ya?"

The closest Tyler could come to a right answer was a shrug, and he wasn't even too emphatic with that.

"Well, fella, I dunno either. Here's what we got. We got Jay and da money gone. We got cops holding one of the guys from da woods over dere in da park. I got nobody else to call to gimme money to get ya back. I can't shoot ya; it'd make too much noise. All I know is mebbe I can find an anchor, tie ya to it, and toss ya over after dark, ferget da whole thing."

Again there was no better answer to give than a shrug, and a beseeching look.

Tyler lay still on the bench seat, watching Tony drink, knowing that the man had only eaten a little bit of fast food since he first saw him over twenty four hours ago. The man was certain to pass out. It would be easy for Tyler to swim to the park and get the hell out of there, if he could untie himself. The man had been wasted when he trussed Tyler, so undoing his bonds shouldn't be too difficult.

Tony returned to his rounds: evil eye to Tyler, swig of booze, peek at the cops. Tyler was certainly thirsty too, but said nothing about it, since that had nothing to do with survival at that time. Survival meant getting away from the maniac that he finally wished he'd never followed.

They heard a distant rumble of thunder. It built slowly into a virtual cavalcade of sound, echoing between all the high-rise condos near them. The boat started to swing as a mainland storm front won its battle over the onshore breeze and brought the daily afternoon rain.

A lightning bolt flashed, and the thunder became more frequent and noticeably closer with each repetition. The wind picked up even more, bringing the smell of pure rainwater, putting a light chop on the bay. As is usually the case, a few loud drops pounding on the boat were followed immediately by a full deluge of water and wailing wind.

Wind turned the boat so that the hatch was downwind, so no rain actually came inside, but the sudden rise in humidity and the lack of through ventilation rapidly made life in the Sea Before quite unbearable. Both men were soon sweating.

The storm was dense enough that Tony gave up on trying to see out the other porthole to the park, so he stared at Tyler non-stop, drank non-stop. The rain and wind were busy creating a mesmerizing cacophony. The greenhouse atmosphere in the cramped cabin became completely stifling. Tony's eyes drooped bit by bit, and he visibly caught himself from falling into a nod a few times before the booze won. Tyler finally had a chance to regain control of his life and sanity.

Chapter 18

Two uniformed officers led a very strange parade of street people through Selby Gardens, and had no idea why. All they knew was that their orders had been to go into the gardens and wait in the northeast corner for a homeless roust. Other policemen would be going in from the waterfront. This was a maneuver that they undertook periodically, and was essentially a population check. Few of the people carried identification, but most were eccentric enough to be easily recognizable.

Different this time was that there was no notice or planning, this was impromptu, and that the officers had been instructed to lead the group into the park was unusual. It was a typically sleepy and docile crowd for that time of day, with the exception of the one woman, an old timer in town named

Jeannie, who had fought, screamed, and kicked like crazy until she was restrained with cuffs, yet still kept yelling that she had to "Wait for her new fella".

The ragtag crew wound their way along the main path in the gardens, one officer holding Jeannie firmly, having to force her to walk. They skipped the main entrance so as to not offend the tourists and stepped over a low chain near the main house.

As they headed down the sidewalk on Tamiami Trail, many of the passing motorists tooted their horns and some waved, obviously in approval of the roundup. Even though the city officials preferred the arrangement, with the homeless focused where they could see them, the general populace was not fond of the continual crowd hanging around at "South Beach", as some local papers had officially penned the area.

The folks that lived there didn't think of themselves as homeless, they felt that they had a home, even going so far as to erect their own statue of junk when the city had commissioned local artists to adorn the entire bayfront with odd, modernistic sculptures.

Apparently, that mockery had been just over the line for the police, who tore it down immediately. There had been an amusing ongoing battle for a while after that: new vertical junk pile appearing in the park overnight, police tearing it down in the morning, oblivious to the fact that it looked better and made much more of a statement than the professional artworks were ever able to.

After about a week, the 'homeless' tired of the game and stopped the competition, mostly because the years of accumulated junk that they had stashed was gone, not because the other stuff was better.

The lieutenant and his crew had headed off of Island Park with their one detainee, and met the marching tribe in the parking lot. As Shake walked, he had been livid with anger. One moment he had been holding post for a seemingly simple operation, and then suddenly felt like he was left holding the bag, instead. Two criminals and two citizens were lost. He had one person in custody on a flimsy aiding and abetting charge.

Once Sonny was in the back of a squad car, Shake attempted the typically futile exercise of questioning the people who had been brought before him.

One of the officers had radioed him about finding Tyler's bike in the woods. When he went around to each of the people, being sure to stand upwind, he got the one answer he expected from each person. 'Don't know nuttin' about no fancy bicycle.'

As he approached Jeannie, one of the policemen who had led the march through the gardens spoke up.

"The woman was talking about having to wait for her new boyfriend."

On a hunch, Shake asked: "Was Tony going to come back for you?"

"Damn right he was," she yelled, "Big Tony's my new man. We did the wild thing all night last night. We're as good as married."

Shake thought a moment, and decided on using her anger to his advantage.

"Didn't he tell you about Susan? She's his long, tall blonde, waiting for him right now."

She lashed out with her right foot and caught Shake a good one in the left shin, hard enough to make him stumble.

"He AIN'T got no Susan," she shrieked, as both of the officers struggled to pull her back, feeling like they had Granny Clampett in their grasp, protecting her moonshine still from the revenuers.

"Big Tony's coming back for ME. Coming back soon as he gets off the sailboat, soon as he gets some more money. Says he'll buy SO MUCH beer and smoke that we'll DROWN in the stuff."

Shake perked up, looked out over the bay, at the hundred plus sailboats moored there. As he thought, he mumbled "Take her in, boys, assault, etcetera."

After her rights were read, she was patted down, one officer losing the seniority race and having to do the awful deed. He found something very unusual for such a person, and handed it to his lieutenant. It was a wallet,

Inside the wallet: Tyler Polk's drivers license and a batch of credit cards. Shake walked a few feet away from the crowd, again staring out at the bay, trying to divine the right sailboat among so many. Plan B started to materialize, simultaneously with a peal of thunder and a few raindrops. Then the raging downpour began. Plan B went on hold.

Rushton Woodside

Chapter 19

The unmistakable sound of a helicopter approached, audible over the sound of the little outboard motor. Jay started jerking his head around, looking behind him, left then right, back again.

After slowing the boat off of a plane, he pulled close to the shore of one of the little uninhabited islands that are scattered throughout Sarasota Bay, and pulled up completely under the cover of some overhanging mangroves. He shut the engine off and held out his hand, nodding towards the grocery bag handles hanging out of Kendra's shorts pocket. She leaned forward just enough to hand him the money, and then shrank back into the bow, worried about what he'd be grabbing for next.

He was a scrawny little man, and she had been trained in several martial arts, fencing, and actual by-the-book boxing, but he had the look of a crazed street fighter - or a Vietnam vet - or probably both. She had been watching their progress around the bay, and knew that he had pulled up to a tiny island choked with underbrush, achingly near her house. There was no running away through the tightly packed greenery, though, no swimming for it when a very sharp propeller might be brought her way. She had seen what happened to the tough hide on a Manatee, akin to the skin of an elephant, and didn't want to find out how her back would fare.

As Jay thumbed through the thick bundles of twenties and hundreds and smiling, a long roll of thunder caused him to jerk his head around. The quickness of his reactions confirmed it for her; he could easily be experienced on the street or in the jungle. They both looked eastward, at the large approaching afternoon thunderstorm that was so common to the west coast this time of year. The clouds were towering into the sky, very dark and ominous. While going back to playing with his newfound fortune, he finally spoke to her.

"Well girlie, this is the biggest wad of dough I've ever seen. It'll hold me for a real long time, if I can keep it away from To... from the guy who called you."

Kendra had a sudden thought.

"If you want, I know where you can get a better boat. One with a roof to keep you out of the rain! You can keep it; it's mine, actually. It's not far from here."

He squinched his eyebrows together and tilted his head sideways before answering.

"So you can get away from me and call the cops? Tell 'em what boat I'm in? I don't think so."

"No, I'll go with you, you can drop me somewhere where I can't call, on a little island like this, keep my phone, use it to call your buddy and catch up with him, he has my friend's phone still, the number is programmed into mine, just push one button!"

She saw from the look on Jay's face that she was rattling on at a rate far higher than the man's comprehension, so she slowed down and started over, enunciating clearly.

"Please, sir. My boat is five minutes from here. There is still time to get there before the storm hits. This little boat will surely swamp in a storm like the one that's coming. You could go find your friend. I will give you my telephone, also."

"Ohhh, I dunno. It's gotta roof, you say? Maybe that's a good idea. As soon as that chopper goes away we'll go look at your boat."

Obligingly, the helicopter stopped circling and headed back to the mainland, the pilot certainly more fearful of the storm than considerate of Jay and his sudden plans.

He managed to crank the Evinrude again, backed out and asked for directions. Kendra led him out of the backwater he had chosen and into the main canal, down between the unseeing mansions which lined it. She forced him to slow down to a crawl, lied to him about how shallow the water was. The start of her still-forming escape plan was to have him drive her Boston Whaler. She wanted him to drive slowly back out of the canal so that they wouldn't ground out on the imaginary sandbar that she was pointing out.

As they headed in, she was judging the closest shelter, something she could swim to underwater on one breath. As a teen, she had been good for almost three minutes in the cold water at St. Moritz, and figured she could go four minutes in her current condition in the tepid canal water.

When they were almost to her docks, she realized her best option was to go for Tyler's dock house. It was a little farther from their path than the other docks, but provided the ultimate hiding place. She would be able to swim right under the closed doors and go back to the bayfront in his Chris Craft, go back and find Tyler. She prayed that she could get the old car engine in it to start without flooding it, but knew that "Venture" was a very reliable and safe craft once running.

She knew her phone would be ruined, but Tyler had been sure to make her proficient on the various radio toys he had mounted all over the dash. It would be a cinch. She was confident that this mess was almost over, and confidently pointed out the Whaler, hanging from davits on one of her docks, had him pull up to the ladder that was necessary during low tide. She automatically tied the bowline off to the ladder, and climbed the rungs while looking back at him.

No lunges on Jay's part, but some very loud and exaggerated kissing noises were thrown towards her rear. She actually blushed and cringed accordingly.

Once she was on the dock, he stuffed the money into the front of his ragged bluejeans and followed suit. He untied the Zodiac while mounting the ladder and pushed it off into the canal, denying her the clue that she wanted to leave for the police in the odd case that anything went awry. She watched it head out to the Gulf in the receding tide, going nearly as fast as they had when coming towards the dock. It shrank out of sight, into the growing mist, around a bend.

Knowing that she had not thought through this part of it, knowing she wanted to avoid taking him up to the house at any cost, she made a sudden decision.

"Sir, we have to launch the boat quickly. The people that I rent the dock from are always home, and I always stop to visit with them when I go out on the boat. We need to get out of here before they notice us, otherwise they'll become suspicious."

He leered at her, causing the second cringe of her life, this time accompanied with goosebumps.

"Girlie, call me Jay, okay? Since we're gonna get to know each other better soon, you might as well use my name. I know yours. It's Kinder. Funny name. Can't we take that boat on the next dock? It's gotta whole roof and doors. This little fiberglass umbrella doesn't look too solid to me. We'll get soaked."

Kendra wasn't about to let him get her cooped up in her Sea Ray, either. "That's the owners' boat. We have to take mine, here."

She flipped a switch on one of the davits, and they started to swing out together over the water.

"This one has canvas side curtains that snap on. We'll be nice and dry inside. It even has a little heater to keep things warm."

Hitting another switch, she dropped the Whaler into the canal, but stopped it when the gunwale was at dock level and climbed aboard.

"Get aboard, Jay, I can drop it the rest of the way from here. Open that locker in the stern. That's where the side curtains are stored."

He obeyed, but kept a watchful eye on her. Once they were floating, she cast off the hooks from the davits, and snapped the curtains into place as they drifted out after the Zodiac, finishing just as the first raindrops hit.

Kendra decided not to tell Jay too much about the controls, just showed him the ignition switch, and set the choke without him noticing. The classic Merc Fifty roared into life for him, sounding throaty since it was made before anybody paid attention to pollution. He started grinning like a maniac at the percolating sound.

Omitting a description of the way the neutral button on the throttle worked, she simply put the boat into forward motion on her own - and did not mention the fact that the choke would have to be released as soon as the engine warmed up enough to run normally. If not, the Mercury would 'load up' and stall, as Tyler had explained to her.

She grew calmer by the second, and even realized that she could immediately call the police from Tyler's landline once inside the dock house. Jay was sure to be stranded on the water within minutes. A sly smile passed over her face. Jay caught it, though, just as her left breast passed over his shoulder as she removed her hand from the gearshift. He, of course, got the wrong idea.

"You smilin' for me? We can have a good time with your boyfriend's money, you know. There's a tiny little island right by Selby where we can park this boat, and go into town anytime we want to. I can getcha some really good pot. We can friggin' live on this boat. Huh?"

She just smiled in response while standing beside the helm, and then looked at the forward curtain that she had only partially closed. Stoop down, go under, long dive, and freedom awaited.

"Jay, I'd like to stand in the bow in the rain going through the canal. Do you mind if I do that?"

"No, Kinder. Just bend over real good when you pass through that little tent door, OK?"

There was no choice but to oblige him, and she managed to not blush this time, and to ignore the kissy sounds that he made. The rain fell steadily now, but not hard. She could see enough to dive, but he wouldn't even be able to see where she had entered the water through the scratched plastic of the old side curtains.

Kendra did love to be in the rain. She closed her eyes, took deep breaths in preparation for her swim, then stretched her arms out wide and flexed them up and down (a little panic-prevention yoga combined with bumping her oxygen flow to maximum level). Getting ready for that last big intake.

She knew that her light clothes were getting soaked, and that the little creature behind the wheel would be getting quite a view, but didn't care. It was almost time. The dock house was near. Turning to give him one last smile as she took the deepest breath she had ever taken in her life, she gave him a Perfect Ten/Bo Derek view of her body, strained against the wet cotton. It was too much for Jay.

As his grip on the throttle tightened involuntarily, he leaned forward for a better view, accidentally ramming the throttle wide open. By a very unfortunate stroke of luck, his elbow bumped the choke button closed. The Merc, just tuned by Tyler, pushed the twenty footer onto plane instantly, as Boston Whalers tend to do when the engine angle and prop pitch are both set up correctly. They were going thirty knots in under five seconds and still accelerating.

Kendra was dumped at Jay's feet beside the console, and she bumped her shoulder ferociously against the hard fiberglass, landing with her right arm trapped underneath her. The forward curtain unrolled in the wind and started to flap noisily. Rain pelted them both.

He kicked at her, nodding his head at the curtain, his eyes wide with the thrill of the sudden ride, his grin ear to ear. She tried to get up, but the deck was too slippery. She yelled to make herself heard.

"I can't get up! Slow down! I'll close it!"

Her confidence wound down as the engine slowed and she finally got up. She could see the dock house way off the stern, along with all of her other neighbors' houses. The whaler entered the main side channel leading into Sarasota Bay now. The rain was picking up. All that was visible was what she assumed were the lights on the Siesta Key bridge, flashing in the distance.

After fighting the plastic zippers closed, she collapsed with her back to the curtain, and looked at Jay. He smiled, and then put the throttle wide open once again. They started bashing their way against the whitecaps being tossed up by the storm, going towards the head of the bay, towards the moorings, towards the city.

Chapter 20

Shake was upset about the rain and the temporary cancellation of his plans. His right foot knew it, and it kept tossing the Malibu sideways on the wet streets despite the factory posi-traction and sway bar package.

He had slammed the Muncie into second at the bay front, and cruised across town with both hands locked onto the wheel, at ten o'clock and two o'clock. Not shifting gears. Burning up John Q's clutch without even thinking about it, as he obeyed each traffic signal on Ringling Boulevard. Driving slowly on purpose – against the best design General Motors had ever made - he was planning a very touchy interrogation of an evil woman whose blood alcohol content probably never dipped below point two-oh.

At the garage, he finally shifted into first, and then blocked the main exit doors as he screeched to a stop. He had been tracking Jeannie's progress by way of the radio, knew she was already inside. He sat dormant for a few moments, breathing in unison with the usual ticks of the cooling big block, then, calmly as could be, opened the door (leaving the keys in the ignition) and sauntered into the back of the station. The way that only cops and criminals used.

Everybody on duty knew what had been going down, as well as the current status of his case. Only nods were exchanged as he passed other policemen in the halls. They all knew that he was on the warpath, and that was never a pretty path.

Shake went straight to his desk and called the head jailer, asked for Jeannie to be put in interrogation room "B", known jokingly by the department as "Studio B". It had everything that a tough case called for: furniture bolted to the floor, no two-way-mirror (to make the subject feel at home), hidden cameras and microphones, one open window for distraction purposes, and – most importantly – a plastic Palmetto Bug super-glued to the wall within plain view of the suspect.

He had bought the fake bug at the gift shop of Selby Gardens on a whim when he first moved to Florida, had used it a few times to scare Cutie, then eventually moved it to its new home, allowing it to intimidate anybody who thought that a jail could be a cozy place. It was a little touch - one that Martha Stewart would probably not approve of - but it always drew the subject's eye. Distraction is a key factor when questioning someone.

Jeannie was making a fuss in the background, being dragged into the room in the adjacent hallway, screaming to the jailers to "Get your damn hands offa my boobs". Anybody who touched her or her boobs would certainly be washing their hands soon.

The desk sergeant buzzed Shake on his intercom, announcing Jeannie's placement, got no answer, but knew that he was at his desk, that he had heard. Hive mentality works well at a station house.

Shake, who had made mental fun of Tyler's meditation the night before, was meditating, with his elbows on his desk, his hands clasped tightly, his fingers laced, his thumbs under his chin, and his index fingers on his nose. There was not much time. The answer had to be gotten before the storm broke. He had to know which sailboat Tony and Tyler were on

That seemed as good a start as any with such a deranged subject. He bolted from his chair, strode to Studio B, slammed the door behind himself as he entered, and then immediately asked her the only question he wanted to be answered.

"Which sailboat?"

"Huh?"

"Jeannie, Big Tony's probably in trouble in this storm. If you tell us which sailboat he's on, we can probably help him out, get him back to the park for you. Get you two lovebirds back together!"

"Sailboat!" she exclaimed. "Jay drove him to a sailboat in the little rubber boat!"

"Yes, Jeannie." – nothing but patience – "He did. We lost track of the sailboat. Which one was it?"

Jeannie got really mean looking as she screwed her face up tighter than the sun had been doing for years. She leaned her head to one side, as if she had just passed out.

"Well, it was a big one. They went there just before you lousy cops came and got us. I dunno...."

As Jeannie faded out like an old black and white television, Shake did a good impression of a double take, hit himself on the temple with the flat of his palm, and excused himself to nobody in particular. He went back to the main desk and asked the sergeant call ABC-7.

The local station's weather cam always scanned the bay from the roof of the Orange Blossom Hotel. Shake had forgotten all about it until then.

He told the sergeant to call the TV station, get a URL, get somebody there to isolate the last hour on disk for them, get an officer online right away to try to trace the Zodiac in the data file. This was in the bag, he thought. Nothing is ever in the bag, he remembered, as he walked back to Studio B and found her in the same position.

"Which sailboat Jeannie? What color was it?"

"They went to the big one. Think it's white and brown. Long one. Got something funny about it, different from the others."

"What's different, Jeannie?"

She shook her head, eyes closed. Wanted her man back, he could tell. Many brain cells later, she finally answered.

"It's the one what has the extra thing on top. The sail stick. An extra sail stick on top of it."

"You mean a double-master, Jeannie?"

"YES! That's what Jay always called it! He knows a lot about boats and that kinda stuff. He always looked at it, saying 'That's the one for me, the double mastiff.'"

Her head drooped again on the last word. Shake turned up his volume and perked her back up for what he figured would be the last time before she was out for the day.

"Jeannie! Did Tony take somebody with him? The guy whose wallet you had on you?"

"Officer! I didn't steal no wallet! Dunno what you're talking about, with the wallet."

Shake took a deep breath - tryed again after a few seconds.

"Jeannie ... Did Tony and Jay take anybody with them when they went out to the boat?"

"Well, yeah. It was the cute beach boy. The fella that bought us breakfast today. Kinda skinny, but he's cute though. Got a funny name, like Poker or something."

"Jeannie, that's all I need to know for now. I'm, glad you turned in that wallet you found today. Do you need a place to sleep? You look a little tired."

"Yes-sir. That'd be real nice, if you got a bed I could lay on for a while. I kinda stayed up late last night, what with meeting Tony and all. We're gonna be married, you know."

Shake left her. She was alone again. Her eyes focused briefly on the cockroach on the wall. She would have gone for it if she hadn't been more tired than hungry. She thought about how her mother always made the best Palmetto Pie in Myakka. Everybody said so, even some snooty horse farmers in Arcadia that her mother cleaned houses for on a weekly basis.

It was cool in the room from the rain, and the sound of it on the window put her right to sleep as the storm lightened and the thunder stopped rolling. She didn't respond while being moved to the cell, put on the cot, sprayed with Lysol. She went to sleep with dreams of the previous night - her night of passion with the man of her, well, dreams.

Shake was already standing behind the desk of one of the younger detectives, watching the bay swing back and forth on a computer screen, waiting for the Zodiac to appear. He called over his shoulder to have someone get the department's Scarab hooked up so he could take it over to the loading ramp at Presidential Park.

The rainstorm had passed.

Rushton Woodside

Chapter 21

Tony was out for sure. Tyler had his chance, but wasn't sure what to do with it. The downpour was turning to a drizzle and the wind was picking up a bit, so he could breathe a little easier now. The weather did nothing for his various aches and pains, though, or for the thirst and hunger that reminded him of a bad day in basic training at Fort Benning.

There was a measurable amount of slack in his bonds, since he had been untied from the tree and re-bound in a hurry by a drunk and stoned man who was also very tired and nervous. The rope that was used felt like a very old piece of nylon ski line that had been in the sun for too long and had become brittle. His wrists and forearms were rubbed raw, and were bleeding from the broken fibers sticking out everywhere, and as he tried flexing against the knot there were crackling sounds.

The condition of the line gave him an idea, but he knew it would take a minute or two, which might be longer than he had. Sitting up on the bench caused a grunt of pain. He tried a light heel kick to it's fiberglass base confirmed his chance. There was no reaction on Tony's part. Stamping on the cabin's deck went unnoticed, also, as well as a clearing of the throat, so Tyler fought his way to a standing position, wincing against the pain.

Backing to a position that put him halfway out of the cabin, he clasped his hands together firmly and pulled them higher behind his back until the scrap of line was drawn tight. He pushed it back against the rough edge of the broken hatch frame. Eyes glued to his captor, he started sawing the line up and down slowly.

This was a noisy job. The scraping sounds resembled a dog growl on the way up, and leather shoes being scuffed on concrete on the downward stroke. With each stroke, though, the sound became more subdued as the line frayed and the rough wood lost more splinters. Every few passes that he made cut some of the rotten fibers of the old rope His hands started to get a little bit farther apart.

The rain was light now, but as the process went on, Tyler's left side got wet to the point of soaked. He didn't let this hamper his project, though. Over and over he continued: dog - shoe / dog - shoe, until his hands suddenly jerked apart and he fell out into the cockpit of the boat, stifling a scream as his sore shoulder hit the hard surface with a resounding smack, reminding him of the baseball bat, of how crazy these people really were.

He lay there, catching his breath, actually pleased that he was now getting wet on the other side, holding his mouth open to catch some rainwater, to quench his thirst. He peeked into the cabin with one eye, the other held closed against the drizzle.

Tony remained in his awkward position, right arm on the table, head on the arm, fat fingers spread loosely around the gun. He was tilted over like a rag doll, snoring the afternoon away, looking like a toddler who had gone way past naptime - except for the gun and the bottle.

Tyler held his place, drinking the dribbles of rain that came his way. The boat was starting to swing again as the sea breeze began to push the storm back. He studied the clutter on the table. His phone was there, probably still holding a charge.

The phone. A quick grab, punch in 911, a brief conversation, and then a dive into the bay and swim ashore, run like hell. That would be the easy out, if he knew where Kendra was. He wasn't sure, but he thought that she might have gone off into the bay with Jay on the Zodiac. The easy out was out of the question for now. Bottom line, he had to get the phone and get away, even if he didn't use it for anything yet.

Once Tyler started to get up, the extent of his accumulated injuries came to his attention. Biting his lower lip and making subtle grunting noises kept the noise down to a respectable level, which allowed him to get on all fours and creep into the cabin, reaching for the phone just as it started to dance away across the dinette table, vibrating from an incoming call. He grabbed the phone and squeezed the button on the side, activating silent mode, stopping the vibration.

Tony didn't stir, thanks to the empty bottle, and Tyler didn't stir, thanks to the fear of God. He took one quiet deep breath. Another. Nothing going on. A peek at the phone showed an incoming call with the local area code, but not associated with the few names of people from whom he would accept calls, and with an imagined shrug he slowly tucked the phone away in his shirt pocket.

This was life or death, dependent solely upon conscious action on his part, not like the unpredictable pit in Viet Nam with bamboo stakes waiting at the bottom - something that is not expected / not like diving under a wooden and canvas cot to avoid incoming mortars at Tan San Noot air base - something that is inescapable. He could keep from being shot or beaten by Tony just through stealth, through patience.

One quiet deep breath, then another. He crept towards the hatch and then into the cockpit, and then crawled onto the swim platform that hung off the stern. Turning around, he lowered himself backwards into the water, feet first. Once he was submerged to his waist he pulled the phone from his pocket and laid it on the platform, slid in, and ducked his head under, which dropped his body temperature twenty degrees in mere seconds. The relief was amazing. His head cleared, thirst and hunger were forgotten. Knowing that he was almost out of this mess, he swore to never do anything so foolish again.

Moments later, Tyler Polk, free man, lay on his back and silently kicked his way towards shore, towards Island Park, holding his phone out of the water. He knew that once he was ashore he would have to call Lieutenant Shake and confess to his most recent interference with the law, after making a much more important call - a call to Kendra.

Chapter 22

Aboard the Boston Whaler, Kendra kept quiet, hunched against the occasional cold spray that pushed through the loose plastic zipper on the front curtain. Jay had slowed down as the wind swell had built into a formidable cascade of whitecaps, and since he had no idea what he was doing, he just drove straight into them at a ninety-degree angle. The Whaler was taking quite a beating, gas tanks straining against their bungee cords with each wave.

The storm seemed to be winning, so he slowed even more, but kept his course. This made things worse as the squared bow of the boat was hitting the swells head on. The storm was actually waning, though, instead. The main problem was that the waves were becoming quite high, as the wind was beginning to pick up after the trailing edge of the rainstorm, and they were beginning to break over the bow of the boat every third or fourth repetition. There was more water coming in than the auto-bailers could handle.

As the rain began to subside, Kendra could see a house on Siesta Key through the clearing rain, and realized they were making no ground speed whatsoever. Second to her life at his hands, she was also concerned that the thirty year old fiberglass whaler might shatter under this terrible beating, and send her out into the gulf, to drown in the heavy waves. She fought her way to a crouch, and crawled back to the center of the boat, knowing that she had to talk Jay into relinquishing the controls.

"JAY - I CAN GET US OUT OF THIS!" she screamed over the constant thump of the hull. "LET ME DRIVE, PLEASE!!!"

When he looked over at her, she saw the fear in his eyes. He had never played with this aspect of Mother Nature, and there was a good chance his pants were now more soiled than before.

She decided to just put her left hand on the wheel, shoulder him off of the captain's seat. He was quite obliging, sliding off to starboard as she slid into the center cockpit. She took that stance Tyler had shown her, half crouch with elbows bent, knees and biceps taking the shock of each wave. As she acclimated during the first few repetitions of the 'squat dance', as Tyler had called it, she knew that when she turned into the face of a wave to end the madness, she might be able to lose Jay off the side. Her concern for his safety was nil.

"WHEN I SEE THE RIGHT WAVE, I'M GOING TO TURN RIGHT," she leaned her head in case he had any directional disabilities, "SO GET OVER THERE ON THE SIDE THAT'LL RIDE HIGH OFF OF THE WATER." This time she leaned her head to port.

Jay crawled around behind her, and sat on the bench seat that ran along the port side of the boat. He clamped his hands onto the seat in anticipation of being thrust up into the air.

Kendra smiled as she saw him bracing himself backwards against the gunwale. She shouted her final instruction

"GOOD - JAY. NOW HOLD TIGHT. I'LL COUNT OFF TO THREE WHEN I SEE THE CHANCE COMING."

She saw him nod out of the corner of her eye. For the next few teeth-shattering slams she stood a little higher, studying the upcoming whitecaps, occasionally glancing towards starboard to visually reinforce her instructions to Jay. She saw a cap-less swell coming up, and mentally counted off the preceding ones. One. Shifting her hands on the wheel. Two. Putting more weight onto her left foot. Three. Pulling up on the wheel to glue her feet to the deck. Then it came.

When she whipped the wheel to port they came down the backside of the last whitecap. There was no immediate affect, as the propeller was wildly cavitating while the bow was sliding down the wall of water. She smiled at the smooth tunnel they were entering and braced herself for the bite of the propeller, pushing the throttle down about halfway. That was enough, she knew, to yank any water skier out of the water.

As the four bladed power prop bit into the water, all hell broke loose. The boat started a gentle enough turn to port, but she immediately straightened the wheel and rode up on the face of her wave. She could hear Tyler's voice from the time he had taught her this emergency maneuver. 'Let the wave steer the boat, just follow it with your hands. I've adjusted your steering cable to zero slack. Let the wave steer you. It's just the same as surfing or wave boarding.'

The boat did become a powered surfboard, but one that was tilted at nearly sixty degrees. She couldn't spare a glance to port to see if she still had company or not. As when she learned how to do this, she was mentally back at St. Moritz, skiing her favorite slope, all muscle tension and concentration, working in a strict tunnel vision mode, constantly making hairline adjustments to the wheel to keep the boat going where the wave wanted it to go.

Kendra was vaguely aware of Bird Key coming up off her starboard beam, and knew that the wind break and shallower water would spread the waves out wider, would give her a chance to level out and drop into the trough, would give her control of the boat. As this happened, as her muscles relaxed and her mind cleared, as the boat leveled off into a smooth plane, she finally took a glance to her left.

She wanted to see the side curtain open with all the snaps along the gunwale popped off, or for it to have a big gaping hole along its base. She wanted to be alone, to pull into an inlet and call Tyler, call the policeman. She wanted, and she was flush with embarrassment at the thought, the man to be dead or gone overboard.

Rushton Woodside

Chapter 23

Miss Georgia Callender stared at the phone after leaving the voice mail message for her nephew Tyler.

"Why wasn't he here to meet me at the gate?" she asked the crowds milling around the airport.

Nobody answered, or even paid her any attention, so she dropped another fifty cents into the pay phone and tried again. Same voice mail greeting, but this one received all the fury she could muster at eighty-one years of age.

"Ty - you knew I was coming for Memorial Day, for the parade you've always bragged about. You were supposed to be here at the airport to meet me. I'll be waiting outside and you better be on your way now, you hear?"

She hung up, retaining her grip on the handset for effect, until she jumped as a hand was placed on her left shoulder. She whirled around, in the mood to give Ty a piece of her mind, only to face a well dressed woman who had been at the gate at Hartsfield Airport, and had been a few rows behind her on the plane from Atlanta.

"Madam," the woman said in a strange accent, "has also your party abandoned? My daughter was to be meeting me here, but, alas, I have of her no sign. I am here to be seeing her home on a Lido."

Georgia drew her head back, having never heard the way that the Europeans switched or omitted verbs and nouns and randomly changed tense when trying to speak conversational English.

"Yep! I'm Georgia Callender, ma'am, and my nephew was going to meet me here to show me where he's been telling me for years to come on down and visit the little small town he found here, though he didn't really find it, my sister Maggie bought him some land here for cows way back before she passed, God keep her soul, and he wound up staying here, so I finally let him buy me a ticket on the airplane, came down here to see the parade they have on Main Street on Memorial Day."

Hedningara Jorgensen mistook Georgia's need to breath for a stopping point, decided to introduce herself as well, and then responded to the last two words since none of the rest made sense.

In her broken English it sounded like: "Pleased, Madam Chawcha. I am Heddie. This Memorial Day, is a holiday? The servicemen who from your country did come to Europe being honored? Uniforms and flags that I have seen on the satellite to do with this Memorial Day?"

Georgia stared, not quite sure what was said, or how to answer. She smiled sweetly, and changed the course of the conversation after a simple non-committal affirmative.

"Yes... Did you say that your daughter lives on Lido Key? That's where my nephew Tyler lives, the one who should have been here to pick me up, but isn't, so I'm going to give him a healthy dose of What For! He told me that it's a little island, so maybe we're heading towards about the same spot. If one of them shows up after we get our suitcases, we could ride together, but if they both keep on ignoring us, we could just hire a taxi cab and ride over there together. Sound good, Sweetie?"

Heddie had to stop thinking about 'what for' and 'suitcases' because it was now obviously her time to speak. She chose the obvious.

"Yes. Taxi to Lido together. Finding our families we would be. My Kendra I saw in New York last. Evil place, that City New York."

Georgia was loosening up a bit now, un-straightening her laces a little, feeling like she had somebody on the porch.

"Yes Ma'am. We'll share us a taxi cab. Show those nogoodnicks what we old ladies can do on our own, eh?"

Heddie was a bit confused about this last statement as well, but recognized the question mark at the end. She held out her elbow in a stately manner and accepted Georgia's arm as they marched off to the luggage turnstile, accosting a porter along the way.

Despite frantic shouts along the line of "Hat box is being mine!" and "The red Pullman. That one darnit!" the porter managed to load all of the luggage onto a cart, and followed the unlikely pair through the doors into the stifling Florida heat, where the rain was just starting its reverse trip, evaporating off the pavement and heading back to the skies.

He stopped, looked at the fifty in his right hand and the single in his left, and turned towards Heddie on the right, actually clicked his heels, and asked her the official, "Where to, Ma'am?"

"Is one car or another we wait for," she replied, "being my daughter or Aunt's nephew. Not seeing daughter or her sportsy car... what is driving your Tyler, Chawcha?"

"Shoot, Henry, I dunno what Tyler's got now cause we don't talk about cars unless he asks me about that old Mercury Comet I keep out to the shed - I mean out IN the shed. He's always trying to buy it from me. Listen up, anyway, nobody's running up to us now saying come on home. Let's just get that yellow taxicab over there to take us off to Lido. We can find our folks from there."

Heddie caught the key words: taxi, Lido, and find, and agreed with a yes that sounded like 'chess'. She marched the porter towards the yellow car, slipping him yet another fifty in the process. They climbed in the back together. The porter did a decent job of having the cab driver keep the two ladies' stuff separated, and between them they managed to squeeze almost everything into the trunk. Just before the driver closed the lid, the porter pulled the two fifties out of his pocket and waved them at the driver with a conspiratorial wink. The driver suddenly no longer cared that his entourage seemed to consist of Eva Gabor and Minnie Pearl.

As Georgia dug Tyler's address out of her purse for the driver, Heddie made her daughter's cell phone ring, unheeded as before, on a small boat crashing through big water. She offered the phone to Georgia, who managed to explain how Tyler always answered, night or day, even when she called merely to complain about kids riding moto-cross bikes on her property (giving great detail of her angst about that), or her bunions, or simply from boredom, all during the time that it took her to dial nine digits and be shown how the SEND button. Heddie understood moto-cross but nothing else.

Tyler had time to give half of an out of breath answer before his aunt cut him off at the pass.

"Ty! Where in the dickens are you? I've been all the way to the city, to that darn confusing airport filled with rude people, on a plane, and am here in your Sarasota where you weren't waiting for me like you said you'd be when we talked on Saturday. You better be at the house now 'cause we're in a taxi and headed that way, and if you're not, you better beat us there, 'cause my bunions are killing me and I need to set up a bit right soon."

Tyler started to cough an answer as best he could, but by the end was talking mountain fast just like she had been.

"Auntie Georgia, I'm really sorry. I've been beat up and kidnapped and nearly drowned and starved by some awful criminals. I just crawled out of the bay after escaping from a man with a gun. Tell your driver to bring you to Island Park and meet me at O'Leary's Deck. That's the seafood place that I told you you'd love to go to. Now I've got to hang up and call the police to let 'em know I got away and call my friend who was looking for me, so ya'll just come on now."

As he clicked off, he realized that she had said 'we', and that he had said 'ya'll', and wondered which cousin she'd brought to 'marry him up to'.

Shaking his head, he called Kendra's cell, causing more unheard rings, left a message then tried her house and left another. A very bedraggled Tyler Polk started walking to the restaurant in the drizzle, just as the local bicycle mounted patrolman came upon him.

The cabdriver, now headed towards downtown, listened to the two accents share some history. His years of service allowed him to understand most of what was said. Glancing at the nodding heads in his rear view mirror showed him that he was the only one.

Georgia Callender & Hedningara Jorgensen were both born in the 1930's - but neither would ever admit to it. They both had the most gentile upbringing available in their regions. Georgia's involved a rambling colonial farmhouse tucked away deep in a valley at the head of the Chattahoochee River in her namesake state, and Heddie's involved an Austrian Baroque castle south of Budapest. While Georgia had spent her entire life within a hundred mile radius of her home, Heddie had traveled the world. Neither had been affected in the slightest by the Great Depression.

Heddie had started with being stashed near Stockholm at the onset of World War II. This was where she met Christian Jorgensen, married his money, bore him two sons, and lived richly, but not happily ever after, until she finally abandoned the sham of a marriage and took off for Switzerland with Kendra in her middle aged womb. With the combined (financial) support of her recently deceased father and her unbelievably compassionate ex-husband, she opened a ski resort near St. Moritz, based around a castle she purchased for a song from the completely broke jet-setting owner.

Georgia's ancestors had settled in the early 1800's near one of the few caches of silver in the southeast. She never married, keeping her share of the family's money all to herself, spinster style, with the exception of the few million she spent creating a private zoo on her mountain top for the local children, and a hang gliding park for the people from Atlanta, which eventually more than made up for both expenditures.

The driver interrupted the monologues by announcing their arrival at O'Leary's, and asking if they wanted him to wait. They answered at the same time with "Yep" and "Chess", and he received one crumpled dollar bill and a neatly folded fifty over his seat back.

He watched the dowagers walk away with their arms linked together, then called his base and explained he had a 'big one' and would be out of service for a while. As he was tucking the bills into his pocket, chuckling at the difference between the two, he heard sirens approach, and then two patrol cars slid to a stop behind him and disgorged numerous uniforms who fanned out into the park. A helicopter roared over him, headed out over the bay, and began to circle slowly back and forth in a long ellipse.

Rushton Woodside

Chapter 24

Lieutenant Shake climbed aboard the ex-drug runner's Scarab while it was still on the trailer in the police yard. He would talk into the mike on his right shoulder and then into the cellphone in his left hand, then repeat. He sat right down in the captain's seat, waving his free hand furiously forward over and over again as if he were pushing a football team to score, or John Travolta to dance harder.

The city's Dodge Ram took off, with sirens whooping and lights flashing, and headed towards the ramp. Shake was so into the moment that he subconsciously dropped his hand to the steering wheel, mimicking the boat's movements as it zigzagged through downtown, still talking animatedly from side to side. On his right he had the ear of the entire force, on his left, just one ear, the pilot of the helicopter. If he had been a cartoon, multi-colored smoke would have been pouring from his ears. His face sufficed, though, in that it was as beet red as is possible for a human to be.

He was a ball of anger that had built layer by layer since he had been called to South Lido the day before. The last problem, the icing on the cake, was having spent twenty minutes watching the image of the bay swing back and forth at high speed, only to find that the Zodiac appeared at the shore on one swing and sped away on the next, with a brief view of cops being too Keystone: slipping in the water, falling down after firing wildly at the little boat, trying to swim after it. He hoped that the TV station would avoid that word, Keystone. As he had run through the halls to the yard, he had yelled aside to the desk sergeant to have the station freeze the images as part of an ongoing. He knew Captain Jenks would negotiate proper presentation.

"Shake! ... Shake! ..." in his left ear, the pilot reporting in, "I've got a bead on both dual masted sailboats. Neither shows sign of occupancy. I'm circling back and forth, advise further action."

Shake barked: "TEN-FOUR! Continue to circle! Hold!", and then concentrated on steering the boat as it looped in front of the boat ramp. He fired up the engines one by one, let them warm up dry as the boat was being backed towards the water. The roar was deafening without the water to dampen the exhaust, ablating any chance at conversation to either side of his head.

Men and women, uniformed and plain, jumped into the boat as it was backed down the ramp, each doing a paratrooper's roll to get out of the next person's way, still managing to pile up. Some were lucky enough to be wearing Kelvar; others started a fresh collection of bruises. That word echoed through Shake's head again: Keystone.

The man who was on the trailer tongue drew his finger across his throat, signaling that the boat was no longer latched on. The water ate up the engine noise, turned it into a vicious growl. The trailer lurched as Shake hit reverse on the dual throttles while most of the boat was still dry. A surge of water over the stern added insult to injury, soaking most everybody.

Shake threw it into forward without pausing for neutral while still going backwards at a good clip. The passengers, some of whom had stood up, all gathered at the stern, in a whole new tangle of arms and legs. With some concerted pushing and pulling, they untangled themselves, and the woman nearest the cuddy cabin starting passing out life jackets. Those that were fortunate enough to get one donned it immediately.

The boat roared towards the bridge. They were mere minutes from Island Park.

Rushton Woodside

Chapter 25

Kendra stared at the torn and gaping side curtain slapping on the side of the boat as she cruised further and further from the rough water. The snaps had all popped off from the weight of Jay's body as she had expected, but he was still there. At least most of him was. Her eyes went to his left foot, tangled in the anchor line which had slid his way as the boat heeled over, then to his right leg, which was draped over the gunwale and twisted and bent in a peculiar manner. Likewise, his arms were straddling the boat; left one inside with hand firmly clutching a seat stanchion, right one bouncing on the water. She became entranced with the action as it would bounce up and splash down, over and over, each repetition sending a little spray into the stern. His head was turned away from her.

She watched the macabre action, glancing ahead periodically to find safe water. She didn't want him to be still in the boat. She didn't want him dead, either in or out of the boat. She didn't want him to exist.

Spotting some glassy water ahead, she pulled gently off of plane, slowed, put the Merc in neutral, turned in her seat, and called his name. There was no response.

It took all of her willpower to get up and put her hand on his back, first noticing the warmth, and then the slight motion as he breathed. Trying his name again got a response. Some choking. A moan. Retching noises. She reached around him and put her hand under his armpit, tried to pull him aboard. He seemed heavy for such a small man. She pulled harder, was rewarded with a lurch, which sent her backwards and put all of her weight into the effort. He rolled onto the deck, his right leg slamming loudly onto the fiberglass. His eyes popped open.

The eyes sent Kendra back to her seat in a panic. She stared at them, not noticing that Jay's right hand had settled on a paddle that had been clattering around the boat - the paddle that she had foolishly not stowed away after her last trip - the paddle that he raised into her face.

"Are y-y-y-you allright, Jay?" she asked.

"Bitch! You turned the other way. Tried ta dump me outta the boat. Lissen up, bitch, Kinder.

You're gonna take us back to Big Tony. Do it! NOW! Turn around and drive or I'll whack you with this thing."

She took a deep breath and muttered: "Okay", turned around to the controls and put the boat in gear, wondering what to do.

"I know where we are," he shouted. "That lil' bridge up there is the one we came under on the way out here. I know it from walkin' over the big one to sleep here sometimes. You better go that way, or I'll whack you but good. Ask your boyfriend Poke. I whacked him good. I like to whack people with things."

At the mere mention of Tyler's name, all of Kendra's resolve disappeared. She turned towards the causeway bridge with tears in her eyes as he gave his last warning.

"Kinder. You just take it nice an' easy, you unnerstand? I gotta get this rope offa my foot while you're driving."

She came gently to plane, feeling the paddle behind her. Leveled off at about twenty knots. The glass continued under the bridge, and past the sailboard park. By the time they were nearing the big bridge, Jay was free and had dragged himself up next to her. They were mere minutes from Island Park.

Rushton Woodside

Chapter 26

Tony had been sweating profusely in his sleep, so subconsciously he rolled his head to the other side. When it slammed onto the table he woke up and his eyes focused on the nearly empty bottle.

"Brea'fast" he mumbled. "Gimme gimme gimme."

Although the bottle nearly toppled over when he grabbed it, he still managed to hold on to it, slide it towards himself, and get it tilted over enough to pour a good bit of its contents into the side of his mouth.

"Bottle...." he murmured to himself, and again "Bottle...pop pop pop pop pop pop."

He took a breath, and in unison with the chopper repeated himself: "Pop pop pop pop pop pop." He got louder as the machine got closer. The next time he spoke he had more force: "POP POP POP POP POP POP."

His head jerked upright, or nearly so. He shut his mouth. The chopper got louder, stayed deafeningly loud for a few seconds, then got fainter, got louder, then fainter again, in cycles.

Each time the sound changed his head leaned one way or the other, like a puppet's head on the pilot's string. Draining the bottle, he pushed himself to his feet, unsteady at best, and stumbled into the hatchway. The onshore breeze had turned the moored sailboats again so he had a direct view of the park, and could now hear the electronic police sirens in that direction.

He saw the chopper appear just barely at the right side of his field of vision, swung around, and headed back towards him. Even though there was a canopy hanging off of the boom to cover the hatchway, he ducked back inside and dropped to his knees on the bunk where Tyler had been, not noticing the absence. As the chopper headed towards him, he heard another strange sound, looked to his right, and saw the Scarab appear at full speed. He didn't have to see the blue lights to know that it also contained cops. With all the time he had spent at the yacht clubs he knew that nobody in their right mind would enter a mooring area like that unless it were life or death.

The chopper stopped before getting halfway to Tony, spun around and headed back the way it had come. The boat was going the same way. Tony suddenly felt like a caged animal, instinct told him to get out. He grabbed his gun and crawled out into the cockpit, clambered over the side away from all the activity, and slid into the water.

Swimming was not one of his fortes, especially with one hand trying to keep the gun dry. He finally shoved it underwater and crammed it under his belt, kicking furiously to stay afloat. He managed to dog paddle past the bow to where he could see a catamaran moored nearby, and headed towards it, He found that when he finally reached it and grabbed onto the mooring line, it slid slowly up over his head as his weight pulled the line into the water.

He hung there with all hell breaking loose too close for comfort. Once the Scarab was throttled down, Tony could hear another sound in the water, the whine of a smaller boat. He pulled himself up a bit and looked out. There was a little white boat with a small roof and flapping canvas headed towards him. It didn't look like cops. As it neared and slowed, he started waving at it, knowing he had about a zero chance where he was. If he pretended to be a downed boater, they would stop to help him, he would flash the thirty-eight, they would get away, and all would be well.

The boat slowed and turned, drifting to a stop a few yards away. Jay stuck his head out, scowling. Tony saw a swim ladder, paddled over and went up it, finally flopping into the boat, yelling, "GO! GO!"

Kendra, still under threat of the paddle, went. She jammed the throttle wide open, with fifty instant horsepower vaulting the half-ton of fiberglass right up on top of the water. She looked back. Neither man had fallen overboard.

Jay was pointing to the right of Selby Gardens with the paddle, towards a little inlet that she knew well, Hudson Bayou. One of her fellow professors at Ringling lived in an apartment there, and Kendra visited her often by boat. The bayou led to a creek that pretty much dead-ended at Tamiami Trail less than a mile inland.

She gladly obliged, having seen the chopper and the Scarab, feeling confident that one or the other would certainly notice her speeding through the no wake zone, follow them, catch up real soon.

Chapter 27

As the officer escorted Tyler down the jogging trail towards the head of the park, he watched the chopper, heard the Scarab coming, and heard the sirens of the cars coming into the park. There had been chatter on the policeman's radio the whole time, which was part of why Tyler had not been able to make himself, or his situation, understood.

The man apparently thought Tyler was one of the homeless, and he looked the part, unshaven, hair unruly, no shirt, no shoes, no ID, nothing but a cellphone. The policeman had taken the phone away immediately, assuming it to be stolen property, and of all that Tyler had said only acknowledged his desire to talk to Lieutenant Shake.

He repeated his one comment: "You'll be talking to Shake soon enough, beach boy. That's him in the race boat. He already passed word along that he wants to talk to anybody we find in the park. No matter what else you are you fit that requirement."

As the man talked, Tyler started noticing something, but wasn't sure, in his groggy state, exactly what it was that he was hearing, just that it was a very familiar sound. Then it hit him, he was hearing Kendra's Merc percolating along at idle. He hadn't heard it come in over all the radio noise. He looked out over the water just in time to see Tony climbing aboard, and then suddenly jerked his arm away from the officer, pointed toward the bay at the Whaler just taking off.

He said: "That's the kidnappers, officer, I know that's Kendra's boat and if it were just her aboard she'd be coming here, not going away so she must have sleazy Jay on board - must have taken the Zodiac off to change boats for him. Then I saw Big Tony climb aboard out of the water right beside the sailboat I was telling you about."

"Whoa down there, buddy," the policeman said. "I've heard both of those names today, they've been all over the radio. Are you sure?"

Tyler looked exasperated. "Yes! That engine is over thirty years old, I know that's her 'cause I tune it myself weekly. I know that sound as well as I know my own mother or My Aunt Georgia."

The man leaned to his shoulder mike, started talking fast. Tyler heard 'Shake', 'Kendra', 'Jay', and 'outboard'. He started to feel relieved. The Whaler could outrun neither Scarab nor helicopter.

"Tyler Polk!" hollered Georgia right on cue as she strutted up with Zsa Zsa Gabor on her arm.

"You look a mess boy and where's your shirt and shoes, running around in public like that it's no wonder you've been arrested. Officer, let that young man go and I'll make sure he ain't - er - isn't out in public looking like a hillbilly no - er - any more."

The ladies had unlinked arms and were flanking the policeman. Georgia had turned her famous waggling finger from Tyler to the officer, and when she stopped to breathe, Heddie kicked in, waving a fist instead.

"Mister policemen, saying daughter's name Kendra. Where is she? What is all fussing about? Is she also under arrested? You are not knowing who is this talking to you, but chess, you will be finding out soon who I am, her mother. Be getting her to me here and now!"

The poor man had backed up a couple of steps under the dual and confusing assault. He looked at each of the three in turn.

"Ladies, calm down, please." he started saying just before the Scarab drowned him out as it took off.

The cop's radio went ballistic with Shake's voice: "IN PURSUIT!! IN PURSUIT!! BILL GET THAT CHOPPER MOVING. ALL UNITS ABANDON PARK. I WANT A CAR AT SELBY. A CAR AT THE ORANGE AVENUE BRIDGE. A CAR IN THE PARKING LOT OF HARBOUR PLACE APARTMENTS. ONE IN PARK PLACE, TOO!!"

The policeman pointed at Tyler, and at a run said: "Don't leave the park. Go to the entrance. Wait for us there...." and was gone.

Tyler was left with the two wet hornets, who gave up all decorum and began to speak to him at the same time. His head went back and forth.

"TY - have you done something improper to this poor woman's daugh"

"Mine Kendra. If you dirty beachy boy have to her something done"

"ter? And tell me now why you're dressed like"

"wrong, you I will have sent to jailers"

"that. No shoes indeed, and bare chested ???"

"for resting of your life, if I leave you resting of life. Mine only daughter is not plaything yours to"

"Your mother, God keep her soul, would just pass all over again if she were alive to see"

"be doing with! Her husband, cousin mine he was, no better than you are being! She left him like leaving you here now she is to deal with mine own self!"

"you like this in front of God and everybody!"

"LADIES!" roared Tyler in exasperation, "Listen to me PLEASE!"

He had backed up each time one of them outspoke the other and took a step towards him. A picnic table pressed into the backs of his legs, and he collapsed onto it with a puppy dog look on his face that would send any woman who spoke any language into submission.

Having their full and suddenly rapt attention, Tyler gave them as abbreviated an explanation of the last day and a half as he could. He gave the key points, being sure to stress guns and blood and baseball bats and bruises. Each sentence caused their faces to droop a little more. Just as he was finishing, the sound of the receding Scarab doubled in volume and changed pitch. The explosion and fireball both occurred right as they all turned towards the water with questioning looks on their faces.

Tyler yelled something he never thought he would say again as he pulled both women into his lap and covered their faces with his arms.

"INCOMING!"

Rushton Woodside

Chapter 28

After all the frustration Shake, was now finally getting his break in this case. Sure he had gone to the wrong sailboat, or at least to an empty one which now had splinters where an expensive teak hatch had just recently existed, but the fact that Polk was safe and on dry land, and that at least one kidnapper and the remaining victim were probably in the bass boat headed across the bay, was his first real good news.

He ignored the fact that half of his entourage was still aboard the sailboat and pulled the Scarab around, throttling up while still turning. Once pointed straight at the soon-to-be-pursued, he opened it up wide. The little boat kept getting farther away as the heavy one slowly built up speed. He figured it must have been going near fifty miles per hour, skipping and darting across the top of the water, as small boats will.

Soon enough he was up to speed, and the situation reversed; he was gaining on them. There was always a feeling of power when driving the race boat, but pursuit doubled that to nearly god-like proportions. His still damp crew had re-gathered in their pile in the stern, since he once again gave no warning before acceleration, and they were not enjoying this near as much as he was.

They could hear him barking the orders for deployment, and from that were able to surmise where they where headed. One male officer, an avid fisherman, yelled something that nobody could hear, and started crawling against the G-force towards the bow, fighting the wet deck, losing ground and starting over again and again.

When he was close enough to grab the base of the captain's seat, close enough to see the frightful grin that Shake was wearing, a grin that was exaggerated by the sixty mile an hour wind, he yelled again.

This time, Shake heard him, though barely. He thought it odd that the officer had come up to say "You fellow" in the busy circumstances, but it made him smile a little bit more. Camaraderie was an integral part of police work, teamwork was always important.

Just after that, Shake heard Bill, in the chopper, yell something just like it over the radio that sent chills down his spine. "TOO SHALLOW!"

Just after that, the water became too shallow for the Scarab. At first it just slowed a bit, the engines growling a little deeper, but then it scooted up one side of a sand bar, flew forty feet through the air in an arc that was very graceful for something that weighed over four tons, and came to a landing, with the bow deep in the sand and the stern sticking up at almost forty five degrees. People flew away at varying trajectories and speeds, scattered to both sides and forward as well.

Everybody had made it out, but they could all hear the engines roaring exhaust into the air, and all knew that no seawater was cooling them. As Bill turned the chopper to come back, he could see the little dots, all swimming rapidly away from the boat, radiating out in all directions.

He just had time to chuckle to himself, noting that if not for the two massive propellers spinning madly at the top, the boat looked just like a football on a tee, waiting for a place kicker, when one engine seized. He saw the fiberglass engine compartment shatter, saw the fireball start when a piece of hot metal pierced one of the fuel tanks, watched the flames grow, then plume straight up, ejecting a nearly perfect mini mushroom cloud.

Bill missed seeing the paddle hit the throttle of the empty Boston Whaler as Jay sent it on its own way up the creek to shatter against the Orange Avenue bridge, missed seeing the three people duck into the mangroves and head south, away from the bayfront proper, towards the Cherokee Park subdivision, loaded with old live oaks, massive Banyan trees, and countless other hiding places.

Chapter 29

Jay quietly led the way, using his paddle as a cane to support his bad leg, pulling Kendra behind by her hand. Tony pulled up the rear. Each was unaware of the others actions as they all patted themselves once. Jay confirmed the bag of money, Kendra her cellphone, and Tony checked his thirty-eight, though he wasn't sure if it would fire after the recent soaking.

They wove their way deeper into the shade of the mangrove trees, where the afternoon sun was barely casting shadows and the air felt cool and damp after the rain. Their trek seemed random, wrought with twists and turns, but Kendra noticed that Jay seemed to know exactly where they were headed, that he never hesitated.

She wasn't aware that Jay was simply following what the Selby crew called the 'South Trail'. They finally worked their way to a moldy brick wall that was obviously very old. He turned right at the wall and followed what was now an obvious foot-worn path, stopped at an area where the wall had crumbled under the weight of a broken live oak branch, let go of Kendra, got down and crawled through.

Everyone was still silent. Tony roughly pushed Kendra down on all fours and prodded her with his foot, not sure himself where they were headed. They crawled through and emerged into a yard that would have had Kendra's Hippie gardener sitting Lotus and calling chants.

This was a known seasonal. The house was always unoccupied from late spring until the fall. The homeless had a mental list of homes like this, passed on just like folklore to only the most trustworthy of newcomers. Hobo style markings, a system of lines and circles and other marks, had been clear on the outer side of the wall, as readable to those in the know as any Realtor's sign:

Occupied November through April
Metal front gate w/electric opener
Fully active Alarm system 24 hours
Lights in house on staggered timers
Lawn service Tuesdays in morning

Housecleaning on every Wednesday
Turn left after wall, go to tree house
Tree house is a completely safe area

Jay had used this place often with Jeannie and hadn't had to stop to read the signs. He led the way along the wall, under the cover of another wall sculpted out of a violet Bougainvillea vine, whose lower branches had died out long ago leaving a virtual tunnel. The tree house was across the open yard from the wall, but the path from the tunnel was blocked from the motion sensors by the Live Oak tree.

Same order up the ladder: Jay - Kendra - Tony, who growled like a cat as he followed the green shorts. Once inside, nobody seemed to want to be in charge, exhaustion was the order of the day. Each person chose a wall away from the entrance, collapsed onto the floor.

Everyone sat and stared a bit, with deep and ragged breaths being the only noise other than the wind in the surrounding trees, and the sound of the few birds that could stay active in the afternoon Florida heat.

Jay finally stood, and retrieved a half-pint of cheap booze that he had stashed in the rafters the day before, hoping to lure Jeannie out for another tryst. He popped the seal and took a deep sniff first, exhaling with a wicked smile on his face.

At the same time, Kendra took a sharp breath, and nearly gagged on the smell. Not the smell of the liquor, but the stench of her surroundings and companions: stale urine - fresh sweat - old sex - mold and mildew and rotting wood. She started coughing, and just as Tony had taken the bottle and had his first swig, started choking. He got up on his knees, put a meaty hand behind her neck and forced her head back with the bottle in her mouth, turning it up full tilt, thinking that he was helping.

She tried to fight off the man's strong arms as she choked even more intently. Booze began spurting around the neck of the bottle, which angered Jay enough to make him stand up and start shouting.

"HEY BIG T!" (each syllable a shout on its own accord) "DON'T WASTE THAT SHIT! IT'S ALL WE GOT!"

Tony growled back: "You're da shit buddy, what wit' leavin' me out onna boat like dat, COPS EVERYWHERE, and then me with some dopey lookin' Beach Boy hanging out inna rain." He was glaring daggers at Jay.

Kendra spurted again, actually said "Blechhh!" as Jay lurched over and yanked the bottle away, clutched it to his chest, collapsed back into the pile of old clothes and blankets where he had first settled. She spat hard onto the floor, deciding that if she didn't assert herself soon she was going to wind up on her back in multiple compromising positions, possibly with a fight going on in the process.

She raised her voice, "Gentlemen! Please stop haggling over your silly bottle. You are both in a lot of trouble with the police. We can stay here and fight, or we can figure out what we need to do that might help you fellows out with the police when they find you."

"Find us!" said Jay in a more reasonable tone of voice. "This place is marked for seven years running. I've made three of them marks myself. Ain't no way John Law is gonna find us here. We got all the time in the world to figger out what to do, Kinder girl."

"Jay, Jay, Jay," shaking her head with each word, "The policemen will find us. They have dogs, they have helicopters, and they have real motive to locate you. You simply can not escape this."

Tony, who had been hit hard by his last dose of alcohol, was swinging his head back and forth to follow the conversation. He heard the words. He recognized most of them, and was proud of that, but the overall gist of the conversation was passing him by. His eyes got bigger as he heard the word dogs (since he had hidden from dogs half of the previous day), and again at helicopters. He had to think about 'motive' though, and that threw him into a state of dehydrated brain lock once he closed his eyes to simultaneously think and listen. He eased back onto his haunches, circled into a lean that sent him crashing against the wall, and went out for the second, and last, count.

Conversation ground to a halt for a bit after Tony's head hit the treated cypress planks that formed the floor of the tree house. Kendra tried staring sense into Jay, who looked at Tony, felt of the bag of money still tucked into his waistband, and pursed his lips thoughtfully, then stared back.

She stared hate while he stared lust. They were both exhausted, from hunger, thirst, and exertion. Kendra really wanted to sleep. Jay really wanted to get drunk. A gridlock ensued as both settled back into their original places, eyes remaining locked.

Clouds began fighting their way back over the bay from the mainland, cooling the air enough for the chicadas and the crickets to start talking about the upcoming rainstorm. Birds joined the conversation. A dog barked furiously. None of the mismatched crew in the treehouse moved an inch. Eyes flitted back and forth, accusing, angry, and jealous.

Chapter 30

If you toss a milkshake into the water, it will float. If you toss Mick Shake into the water, he will both float and cuss. He did a fine job of proving this, doing an impressive backstroke while blurting out a stream of obscenities which would blush your average sailor.

Once his mouth stopped working, he sighted on the sun and turned until he was heading east, towards the mainland. Without a glance around to see where anyone else was, he issued orders for his complement to follow him and then started giving specific instructions to many of the officers who had been aboard. One of these was to get to a phone and call headquarters to have them get the artist over to Tyler immediately, 'if not sooner'.

Most of them were already ahead of him, swimming towards the sea wall that protected the ancient Bo tree at Selby Gardens. One officer was already over the wall helping others up when Shake was grounding the back of his head against the bottom. Everyone gathered under the tree. Yet nobody was meditating as the tree might have wished...

He flipped over, got up, and leaped over the wall with no help, started splashing his soggy Jansens along the paved path towards the rest of the world, towards those who had not just been airborne.

The entourage followed. All radios were wet, ruined, and silent, so it was a grumbling and motley crew that tramped out of the main entrance to the gardens in silence, much to the dismay of the two blue-haired volunteers who backed away from and then dove under their admissions counter at the sight.

Once on the small piece of Palm Avenue, resplendent with its original brick paving, Shake saw a marked car, splashed into the passenger seat, and commandeered the radio, which was currently chattering with news of the crashed Boston Whaler, empty and in pieces. He broke in and got the location, repeated it to the patrolman in the car, and then called for the dogs, and for another flush of the homeless camp. He then called Billy, asked what he had seen.

"Nothing, Shake," Billy replied, trying not to laugh, "I was watching you guys coming up after me. I lost track of the boat for a minute, then when I looked back, it was headed towards the bridge. I assumed they were still aboard, so I wasn't paying any attention to the sidelines."

Shake barked at him: "Well, get circling Billy Boy, and don't come down until you spot them. I'm not sure how many people were on the boat, but at least one is a victim."

"Roger!"

Billy clicked off his mike, and then chuckled a while as he started south, trying to stare into the impossibly thick forest below.

Shake arrived at the crash scene, chagrined by his own problem of a few minutes before. He knew that even if he caught his perp in a hurry, he would never live down the flying boat. Jenks would certainly never let him forget, and that one guitar-playing officer would probably write a little ditty about it.

There wasn't much to see. Three large pieces of styrofoam-packed fiberglass were floating back out to the bay. One large piece was pointed at the sky as it bobbed. A gas/oil mix stain spread over the water.

Shake paced while waiting for the dogs. There were two officers in the water trying to retrieve the center portion of the boat so the dogs could get a scent. The men struggled a bit, couldn't get it to go against the receding tide, and finally started kicking it towards shore instead.

He stopped at the car and called back in, asked for Captain Jenks, and explained the situation as calmly as possible.

The K9 crew arrived. Shake had the dogs scent the boat's drivers seat, and sent each dog off on separate sides of the bayou, dragging their handlers through the tangled shoreline towards the bay. He ousted his driver, and took the car back to the park himself. He intended to give Tyler Polk a royal reaming, and then to send him off to the station on charges of obstruction and interference, even if he had nothing to do with the boat fiasco. He certainly had a lot to do with the whole mess, and if Shake didn't bring somebody in other than a toothless hag, he would be getting his own royal reaming from Jenks.

Chapter 31

Georgia would have pulled Tyler along by the ear if she had been taller, but she settled for keeping her hand gripped tightly onto his wrist as they walked towards O'Leary's Deck, the restaurant at the head of the park.

She saw that there was indeed a deck outside facing the bay, and marched onto it, then sent Heddie to remind the cab driver that they were waiting, and gave her another dollar for the man.

There was a guitar player under an awning on the deck, singing a Jimmy Buffet song, something about a pirate. Tyler, having just left his own version of a pirate, didn't appreciate it.

Georgia went inside the restaurant and ordered a burger for Tyler, bought him an iced tea and a souvenir T-shirt. She started giving him a hard time as she came through the screen door, letting it slam behind her. He knew he was in trouble if she was abusing an innocent door.

"Ty, you've upset me and that nice Henry woman and you've lost her daughter, of all things to do. I've never known you to act so foolishly as to go chasing after criminals like you're the sheriff like your cousin Ron over in Dahlonega. I just can't believe all these shenanigans. If your mother, God keep her soul, were here today she'd give you what for, and I'm just gonna have to do it myself to do honor to her and your daddy, so you better lissen up...look, Ty, here come some policemen, so I'll have to finish up with you later. Put this shirt on. It's got a little sailboat painted on it. You won't look like such a hooligan if you're wearing a shirt. You must not be under arrest if they left you here with us. Is he under arrest, Officer?"

The uniform turned to look at Shake, who would do all the talking as senior man onsite. Shake had seen Georgia's body language and heard the last of her little speech. He figured that Tyler would be getting enough grief from her, and changed his mind about the arrest. He could deal with Jenks somehow.

"Ma'am," very politely, "Mr. Polk is not under arrest for any crime, though he could be for interference."

She poked Tyler in the shoulder with her wagging finger, hitting Jay's favorite spot, making him wince.

Shake continued, "Mr. Polk, we have an artist on the way over. Can you remember what the two men looked like?"

"Yes sir. Pretty well."

"Good, now I'm going to tell you one more time to stay out of police business, stay away from this park for the day. Work with my artist, and go on home. Your . . . " indicating Georgia.

"Aunt, officer." she clarified.

"Your aunt can take care of you. I want you at your home until we get some resolution on this case. Is that clear?"

"Yes Sir, sir."

Georgia spoke again: "Officer, the mother of the kidnapped girl is due back here any minute. What can you say to her about her daughter? Can you calm her down?"

"Yes, ma'am. That's one of my specialties. I've worked homicide for most of my career. How much does she know about the situation?"

"Lieutenant Shake," said Tyler, "she pretty much knows everything. I've filled her in from the beginning, though there is some communications problem. She's European and has marginal control of English."

Shake nodded slowly. Since coming to Sarasota, he had dealt with people from other countries who had a different perspective of the law. Most of them thought that he was nothing but a servant, and gave him exactly that much respect.

He saw the pair look past him to the path leading up to O'Leary's, and turned to see Heddie striding towards them. He recognized the walk of self-perceived royalty, cringed slightly, and then turned to face her, his hands clasped deferentially behind his back.

"Hello, madam," he began, "I understand that Miss Jorgensen is your daughter, and ..."

Shake was interrupted by the fact that Heddie kept walking towards him and grabbed him by the upper arm. She began shaking poor Shake too violently for such a demure looking woman. With each push she uttered one word, and with each pull she yanked his face right into hers.

"YOU - MUST - BE - THE - MAN - WHO - HAS - ALLOWED - MY - ONLY - GIRL - TO - BE - STOLEN!"

Halfway through her statement Georgia walked over to her and put a hand on her free wrist, and one on her back. She was trying to speak to her, to calm her, but had never seen such anger in a woman before, and was having a hard time making herself heard.

Shake fortunately had no need to attempt a reply, as Heddie broke into dramatic crying when she released his now bruised arm. She folded into Georgia's proffered embrace, sobbing violently.

Georgia made cooing sounds as if to a baby, tossing in a "there - there" now and again. She led Heddie to a bench on the deck, sat with her, and pulled her to her breast, rocking.

The sketch artist arrived as the women did woman stuff. Even with a large part of Tyler's spare time spent keeping track of technological advances; he was surprised to see a nerdish individual with a Thinkpad under his arm instead of a sketchbook.

They had Jay pegged almost instantly, as he only had three main features: a darkly tanned and wrinkled forehead, an obviously bent nose, and a beard that might or might not have been trimmed this year. The artist brought each feature up from a database as Tyler gave his description. The composite looked like an angry and dirty Santa Claus.

Tony took a bit more time, looking at first like Homer Simpson, and then Dean Martin with a weight problem as wavy dark hair was added. After a couple of tweaks to the nose, Tyler yelled: "Yes - YES. That's him exactly!"

The little party broke up. Shake was handed an instant print of both criminals to take to the police station. The artist hurried off to the ABC-7 studio to get the pictures displayed on a special alert, which Captain Jenks had already arranged.

The victimized trio walked to the taxi, Heddie in the middle.

Tyler gave the driver Kendra's address. As her best friend, he had a key to her home and her alarm code. They rode in utter silence. As they crossed the causeway, he stared out the left window, watching the rain clouds coming back over the Sarasota Bay, unsuccessfully trying not to cry.

Chapter 32

Kendra figured her best chance was to get the two men separated. She'd seen animosity between them, and wanted to put it to work for her benefit.

She leaned forward and whispered to Jay: "Do you really want to give up half of the money? That's enough for you to live quite comfortably for a long time. Do you even think that Tony will give you half? What if he just takes it all and leaves you behind?"

Jay didn't answer, but his eyebrows showed her that she had gotten through to him. He nodded and put his finger to his lips in the shhh motion, then rummaged a bit in his pile of rags. He tossed a few things out the door, stood, pulled out his now wet bag of money and tossed a small handful of bills on the floor beside Tony, then headed for the ladder and motioned for her to follow.

They climbed down the ladder, with Jay stopping to pick up the strewn clothing at the bottom, and went back through the Bougainvillea tunnel to the hole in the wall. After both had climbed through, he handed her two of the pieces of clothing, and proceeded to strip.

Kendra turned away, slid the stinky pair of sweatpants on over her shorts, nearly gagged as she pulled a polo shirt over her tank top, and waited for some signal that he was ready.

"You can turn around now, Kinder. I wouldn't have figgered you for the shy type. We'll have to fix that later."

He grabbed her hand again and led her further along the trail they had used before. They skirted around some houses at the water's edge, continuing south, away from all the activity. Billy was circling nearby, they could just hear his engine, but Kendra knew nobody would be able to see through the tangle of trees.

They crossed a dead end street walking side by side at a spot where one homeowner had walled his property to the waterline, then followed the path for a few more minutes. The sound of the helicopter faded away. Jay felt good about their escape.

Eventually, they reached the end of the trail, a spot where they had to walk up a little residential street to Osprey Avenue. Jay turned right, and they strolled down the sidewalk. He had decided to stop at a little gas station where he could get some supplies, and go camp at an empty lot he knew of near the Siesta Key bridge.

He explained his plan to Kendra. She half listened, but was trying to work on a plan for herself, some way to get the attention of the passing motorists to let them know she was in trouble. He still had a death grip on her right hand. She figured if she tried waving with her left, people would just think that she was crazy as well as pitiful looking.

"Passing!" yelled a woman on a bicycle. The couple stepped aside for her to go by. As Kendra watched her recede into the distance, and saw Jay mesmerized by the sight of her bike shorts accentuating each buttock as it flexed in turn, over and over, she found her answer.

Kendra slowly but surely started falling back from beside Jay, inch-by-inch, feigning tiredness, until she was a half pace behind. She put her hand on her hip, hooked her thumb under the waistbands of both the sweatpants and her shorts, and slowly pulled them down, a little more with each step. One side - then the other.

Soon the elastic was hooked beneath the curve of her bottom. Her thong had long since crept out of control and sight, so she was offering a full moon. The first horn honked, then another. As the cars passed, most of them had waving arms hanging out the windows.

Jay wondered why people were honking, turned to look at the cars coming up behind them, but from his angle, he couldn't see why. He went back to enjoying the cool afternoon breeze under the cloud cover.

Kendra found the breeze disconcerting, wanted to reach behind herself and put things back where they belonged. A blush brighter than any sunset worked its way from her neck to her forehead. But she stayed calm, knowing that someone would object enough to call the police.

Sure enough, a very prim and proper female attorney drove by in her Mercedes, gawked, blushed herself, and then called the main non-emergency police number, which she kept in her cellphone.

The lawyer described the obscene atrocity and gave an apt description of Jay to the station operator (who had just watched Shake post color copies of the sketches). The operator yelled his name as loud as he could through the door to the squad room.

Kendra was minutes from freedom. . . by virtue of an obscenity arrest as far as she knew. Her 'runway walk' incongruously reminded her of Susan and her display on the beach the day before, and decided that the first thing she would do once free would be to pay a visit to the poor woman. She knew Tony wouldn't be doing that anytime soon.

Chapter 33

Tony woke up once again to the sound of a chopper circling, and looked around the interior of the tree house, again disoriented in respect to space, time, and companionship.

One deep breath, two. A flash of fear made him into a disoriented, but standing, man. He finally began remembering the events of the day, and the day before, and the night before that when he was simply doing a "pickup" as he and Susan called it.

Feeling like a hunted and treed animal, he made for the ladder, just barely catching a glimpse of the cash at the last second. He scooped it up, along with a handful of anger at Jay's having copped out on him.

Somehow, in his alcoholic daze, he remembered his way through the tunnel, through the wall, and to the trail. He saw Jay's discarded clothing, made an un-educated guess, and headed off in the same direction.

When he also had to skirt the walled mansion, he saw the fresh muddy footprints on the street, followed them across, and managed to pick up the trail again. He heard the chopper, but could tell it was headed away from him in a hurry. He didn't know that Billy was responding to Shake's call to get to South Osprey where cars would soon be surrounding Kendra and Jay.

Tony intended to find them himself, use his last bullet on the traitorous Jay, and reclaim Kendra and the money as his. In his dementia, he imagined making her his new moll, his new partner. He thought about how fine she would look on the docks. After his years with Susan, he was on the prowl again, a tomcat in heat and cruising.

When the trail ended, he also walked up to Osprey. There was a long rain puddle in the gutter of the side street, and he used that to get the mud off of his nearly ruined shoes, unintentionally foiling the dogs that would be coming along soon.

He noticed that the chopper had stopped moving away from him, which gave him a scare. It was gaining altitude rapidly, perhaps, he thought, to get a better view. He ducked off onto a side street, heading towards Tamiami Trail, knowing, since he now had his bearings, that he was almost back in his own neighborhood.

Once he got to the main road, he discovered, as he had suspected, that he was close to one of his favorite haunts, the Cabana Inn. He hadn't counted the money in the tree house, but knew that there had been several twenties, so decided to risk being seen long enough to stop for cold beers and a couple of bar burgers. As he neared the bar, he heard sirens, causing him to run the last block.

He burst through the door out of breath and saw to his relief that the place was deserted. Within ten minutes, he had downed three beers and two burgers, tipped a twenty on a twenty-dollar tab, and headed out the back door into the approaching darkness of the second rainstorm of the day.

Tony continued south, closer to home, though he knew it would have been foolish to actually go to his apartment. There were dark bars every few blocks, and his plan was to drink his way south until nightfall, then acquire a car, and find a new city, this time without Susan. He accepted the fact that there was little hope of finding Kendra and Jay.

Rushton Woodside

Chapter 34

Shake had been the first to arrive in the area, and drove past Kendra's little display with a chuckle at her ingenuity. He knew that the residential area involved could make it difficult to catch Jay if he ran, so had arranged a net with several cars and bicycle-mounted officers, with Billy hovering way overhead as an observer.

With the Malibu poised at a stop sign that led a side street onto Osprey, and the radio going non-stop, he directed his officers into position.

He planned to use two bicycles, each coming from opposite directions on the sidewalk. The one in Jay's line of sight would stay to one side, then swerve right into him at the last second with a rolling body slam, hopefully not harming Kendra. The other officer would time her arrival from behind the couple to coincide with the slam.

Three seconds and one pair of handcuffs later, a felon would be in custody and the second abductee would be safe and sound. Rounding up Tony should be easy since most of the County Sheriff's department was now also involved.

Shake could see the odd couple walking towards him a block and a half away, one using a paddle as a cane, the other with her ass hanging out. As soon as the road was clear for him to turn left and head towards them, he signaled the first bike out from beside his car onto the sidewalk, and radioed the second to begin her trip.

He pulled out after the bike went past, staying behind it a couple of car lengths, driving much slower than the car was designed to. He felt the collar this time, knew it would happen smoothly even if Jay had a gun, which was the only uncertainty. Things would go too fast for a gun to come into play anyway.

A marked car had blocked the road a few blocks north, and Shake held back the northbound traffic by driving so slowly. Once the bike was within a few pedal strokes of Jay, Shake pushed in his clutch, slammed the indestructible Muncie shifter into first, put the gas pedal to the floor and popped the clutch. He veered left as he started burning rubber, headed towards the sidewalk across the center of the roadway, distracting Jay and Kendra just as the two bicycles did their work.

The Malibu skidded to a stop with the door already open, right beside the struggling crowd, and Shake jumped out and cuffed Jay himself.

Kendra, forgetting about her distraction in the heat of the moment, ran up and threw her arms around the lieutenant, sobbing thanks. The female officer from the second bike politely came up behind Kendra and adjusted her pants for her.

As Jay was being loaded into the back of a patrol car, Kendra recovered enough to ask Shake about Tyler. She was ecstatic to learn he was allright, and shocked to be reminded of her mother's arrival in Sarasota.

She pulled the telephone out of her pocket as Shake told her that he would take her home as soon as she was ready. While he walked away to talk to the driver of the patrol car, she called Tyler's phone, crying happy tears.

Rushton Woodside

Chapter 35

Tyler and the ladies watched the bust in real time by virtue of ABC-7's news chopper, which had been allowed to hover within camera distance. Captain Jenks had approved this, to get some good press to offset all else that had happened in the last two days. He had finally admitted to the media that all of the events, the murder of Petrosky, Susan being shot, both kidnappings, and the wrecked boats, were connected. He had to show the connections to stress the importance of getting the artist's sketches broadcast in the continual emergency reports that had been running.

Heddie lost her cool when one of the emergency reports was interrupted by yet another one, a shaky camera view of Jay's back and Kendra's backside, with a screen-in-screen shot of the station's news producer blushing her way through a description of Kendra's daring escape plan.

"Chawcha. That is daughter mine Kendra and her bottom on the television set!" shouted Heddie.

Georgia shouted too, "Tyler, turn away from that TV screen right now. This ain't - umm - isn't proper."

Tyler turned, but had to watch the action out of the corner of his eye. He saw it all, Shake and the bikes all converging, the handcuffs going on, and then Kendra pulling her cellphone out of the pocket of her shorts. When he saw that, he dove for his phone just before it rang.

"KEN, are you okay?"

"Oh Tyler. They only scared me. There never was time for them to do anything else. Do you know if they've caught Tony yet?"

"No, Ken. They've got his picture all over the TV, though. It's only a matter of time. Listen, your mother is here, and remember I told you that Aunt Georgia was coming? They arrived at the same time. We're all at your house. I'll come get you. Where are you on Osprey?"

"Lieutenant Shake is here," she said, "He's going to bring me home as soon as I make an official statement. Just wait, Lover, I need a hug real bad. I'll make him hurry."

They said their good-byes, each with tears in their eyes. Tyler dropped his head, eyes closed, clutching the phone tightly in his hand. Kendra stripped off the filthy clothing, and walked to the Malibu with Shake, who put the blue light on the roof and switched it on, hit his siren, then hurried her home, home to her family, while she made her statement into his digital recorder.

Rushton Woodside

Chapter 36

After dropping Kendra off, Lieutenant Shake headed back to the south side of town to join the dragnet. He had gotten word on the radio that the dogs had found a scent, and that they tried to go two ways at once upon reaching Osprey Avenue. One dog was obviously on Jay and Kendra's trail, so his handler headed back to join the other, whose dog was whining and wandering up and down the long puddle that Tony had walked through. Both dogs did this routine for a while. The handlers finally gave up and went back to their car.

Shake had issued an order for all pedestrians on the south side to be stopped and questioned, be they homeless and wandering, residents and jogging, or one of the many bicycle commuters that populated the sidewalks that time of afternoon.

Many people were questioned, but none had seen anything important, except for one lone bicyclist who mentioned having seen a half naked hooker walking down Osprey Avenue with a 'street bum'.

Shake had one officer distributing copies of Tony's picture to local convenience stores, restaurants, and bars. One store acknowledged having sold cigarettes and a lighter to him, and a check of the register tape showed him to have been on Tamiami Trail at about four p.m.

As shift changes came due for the force, Jenks authorized the rare overtime to any and all officers, so as to continue the search. There were almost a dozen takers, most of whom were instructed to go plainclothes, and were issued bicycles.

A watch was put on the address on Susan's driver's license, an apartment adjacent to the mall at Southgate, easy enough to watch from the parking lot.

The FAA had strict requirements for helicopter pilots, so Billy was free to go as soon as his shift replacement arrived. This was fine by him, as he considered himself more of a pilot than a policeman, and besides, he and three other officers had a band called the 'Blues Police', who had a happy hour gig at the Classic Wax Bar & Grill that afternoon.

While the search went on, they drove straight to The Wax, not having to stop for the usual pre-gig pot smoking session that caused many bands worldwide to arrive late for jobs, fumble through setup, and not get into tune until the third or fourth song.

They were unloaded, setup, and playing right on time. Being newly formed, they didn't have a strong following yet, but played heartily for the dozen or so people who were chasing their daily happiness. Being straight and sober, they also played well, so the owner of the club left her door propped open for the draw of tight blues rifts pouring out onto the sidewalk.

This was their first gig at The Wax, so the band watched each new arrival to the club closely. Everyone who came in nodded his or her head at the band in approval. Fans fuel a band like wind fuels a fire, so they were going strong with their version of "Give Me Three Steps" when a very bedraggled looking Tony DeCastro stumbled in.

Tony had never understood music, so he didn't look at the band and nod. He went straight to the bar instead and nodded to the bartender while pointing at the bottle of Budweiser in the adjacent customer's hand.

Beer in hand he turned to watch the band, but didn't pay attention to the very authentic looking Sarasota Police T-shirts.

Two by two the band members shared looks, and nodded, gathering the consensual opinion that they all recognized Tony, and had a bust coming up. They segued into The Allman Brother's "Whipping Post", a song sure to whip any audience into a frenzy.

Billy, the bass player, stepped off the stage to stand right in front of the door, acting as if he needed more room for the driving bass line that controlled the song. The guitar player, Chip, who had a wireless transmitter on his Les Paul, stepped out onto the dance floor when it was time for the extended guitar solo. As he finished, he moved off towards the aisle that led to the back door.

This gave Paul, the keyboardist, room to pull his mic from its stand and walk out onto the floor for the final refrain. As with any good band, everybody always knew what was going to happen next. The last word in the song was usually "dying'", but there was going to be a substitution this time, and that would be the signal. Chip was no longer playing his guitar; he had the strap off his shoulder and the neck of his guitar held firmly in both hands. He was sidling towards Tony.

Paul was wailing to just drums and bass:
"Like I been TIED to the Whipping Post
            TIED to the Whipping Post
                TIED to the Whipping Post"
"Good Lord I feel like Iiiiiiiiiiiiiiiiiiiii'm . . ."
"BUSTED!"

Tony didn't see the Les Paul coming. He didn't feel the twenty-two pounds of mahogany impact his skull, or the concrete floor rush up to meet his face. He didn't come to until long after he was in a holding cell downtown. When he finally opened his eyes, the first thing he saw was one Detective Lieutenant Michael Shake smiling at him from a metal folding chair, in the hallway outside of the cell, humming an Allman Brothers tune, spinning Tony's thirty-eight around his index finger.

Rushton Woodside

Afterword

Tony was given a life sentence, and Jay a twenty-year term. Jeannie found another boyfriend, then another, over and over again...

The Blues Police, despite having earned the respect of the community in general, was never asked back to the Classic Wax.

Susan Kane was released from the hospital a week after admission, with minimal scarring and no cocaine left in her system. Kendra took her straight back to Lido, where she wound up being half-maid and half-roommate, and found that the primo pot that the caretaker surreptitiously grew there kept her from wanting alcohol or hard drugs. She also found that hippies make much better lovers than thugs.

By Memorial Day, Heddie and Georgia had become the best of friends. Heddie rented a motor home and hired one of Kendra's students to drive them to Biloxi for a gambling spree.

Tyler proposed to Kendra, and they were married on the beach before the two matriarchs took off on their trip. It was a simple affair, yet grand in its own respect, due to perfect weather providing an exquisite sunset, complete with green flash.

They honeymooned on Tyler's abandoned cattle ranch in DeSoto County, east of Sarasota, ignoring the tumbling-down farmhouse for a small and cozy tent. Each morning they biked to the Peace River before dawn, where they launched their kayak built for two. They would paddle upstream just before sunrise, when the pre-dawn glow was beginning to appear over the swamps and the morning breeze cooled the hot night.

Each day they would photograph the flowers opening for business, make videos of the flurries of butterflies that flocked to the flowers, and recorded the calls of the mourning doves.

In late July, on the last morning of their extensive honeymoon, the day before Kendra was due back to work, the usual morning symphony was marred by a strange noise.

They stared quizzically at each other. Tyler whispered that it sounded like a wooden baseball bat being used very successfully with a pitching machine, like someone had mastered a perfect batting average. Kendra suggested a tree being chopped down by a professional lumberjack.

Silently pulling the kayak ashore, they crept into the tall grasses that grow under the massive live oak trees, and went off together to investigate whatever was happening on their property - without calling the county sheriff first.

THE END - For Now

Learn more about Tyler and Kendra Polk's next adventure in "Peace River Runaway" to be released in early 2005.

You should have a second copy of "Sarasota Bay" for your next out of town guests to read.

Certainly someone you know needs a picture of some sunny weather in their Christmas Stocking this year!

Visit your local bookstore, log-on to Amazon.Com, or just simply mail a check or money order for $9.95 ($7.95 each for 5 or more copies) to:

LIDO Press, Inc.
Post Office Box 1257
Sarasota, Fl. 34236

(Florida residents add 7% sales tax)
(Delivery is only available in the Continental United States.)

Shipping and handling to a single address is FREE!!

Rushton Woodside - born and raised in the deep south in the 1950s - traveled the country for a few decades, and worked at such diverse locations as a waterfront golf resort, a yacht club, a pool hall, and two bars. Not only has he made presentations in board rooms of Fortune 500 Corporations, he has also worked in warehouses. His diverse experience includes backstage work for the original Allman Brothers and many other Atlanta based bands. He then spent seven years of his life writing COBOL programs and operational manuals.

He finally settled down as a bookseller on Lido Key in Sarasota in 1992, and is still a bookseller and a musician, as well as an artist and a graphic designer. A back injury recently put him in the writer's seat. This is his first published work of fiction.